Our Lowry Sketchbook in Colour

An anthology of new creative writing to commemorate the
50th anniversary of the death of L S Lowry.

Table of Contents

Introduction

This anthology, focusing on the celebrated painter L S Lowry, is intended to commemorate the fiftieth anniversary of his death in February 1976. The varied contents attempt to piece together our own 'word pictures' of the man whose art was often regarded as strange – and certainly different.

However we have come to regard his works, Lowry certainly broke the rules of painting with his strange little figures. Our collection includes short plays, stories, memoirs and poetry – as well as speculative pieces aimed at shedding some light on Lowry's thoughts and inspirations as he went about his daily life in and around Salford and other places in the Greater Manchester area.

'SWit'CH' is the name of our writing group, which is mainly based in Swinton. So Lowry was our local artist. The varied contents seek to explore his life, his world and his unique style of creativity.

We hope you enjoy this anthology of writing dedicated to his memory.

Foreword

By Derek Antrobus, former Salford City councillor, Swinton North ward. , is a local historian and former deputy editor of *the Swinton and Pendlebury Journal.*

When Laurence Stephen Lowry died in 1976, the *Swinton and Pendlebury Journal* ran a brief, rather flimsy obituary, as if written by someone who was unacquainted with Lowry's work and unaware of the artist's impact on the town. Instead of the news of the great man's death being the subject of in-depth and extensive treatment, the task was given to the most junior member of staff who confined the illustrious career to a few sentences. I confess I was that callow, shallow journalist.

Fifty years on, I have the opportunity to put things right thanks to the endeavours of SWitCH – Swinton Writers in t'Critchley Hub – who have produced a wonderful anthology of new creative writing to mark the 50th anniversary of Lowry's death entitled *'Our Lowry Sketchbook'*. Edited by Sylvia Edwards, the book illustrates how deep the influence of Lowry reaches into the hearts and minds of Salford folk.

I was made aware of his importance by a former Swinton and Pendlebury Borough councillor, one Theophilus George Harrison, who explained that the actor Ben Kingsley had lived there; a neighbour was one-time TUC President, Marie Patterson and next door was L S Lowry. I learnt from George that an important official of the General Union of Loom Overlookers, was also their neighbour. That official was George himself who could possibly have been the inspiration for the bothersome Labour councillor depicted in the 2019 film Mrs Lowry and Son.

Les Hough, leader of Salford City Council at its 1974 inception, was a no-nonsense socialist. In internal budget

3

meetings, he would always ask whether the council could sell a few Lowry paintings to help alleviate child poverty or address housing squalor. After all, he argued, the artist's work was of no value: 'I'd have had my backside tanned if I'd drawn something like that at school.' And yet it was the work of Lowry which was so influential in the regeneration of the city's image. Les had led one of the UK's most successful dockland redevelopments at Salford Quays. The city's Lowry collection was transferred to a dedicated gallery in the Quays complex, which includes two theatres, studios, a restaurant, bar and café. I cannot believe that Les was not briefed about this project which he would have endorsed wholeheartedly. The Lowry opened in 2000 – the only millennium project to finish on time and within budget, it was boasted – and is now among the top tourist destinations in the North-west. So keen were the city's movers and shakers to exploit Lowry's global appeal, that one of the first performances at the theatre was a ballet *A Simple Man* about the life of Lowry.

So embedded is the name of Lowry around our city that it can lead to confusion. I was once asked to welcome delegates to a conference at the Lowry Hotel only to find a significant number were waiting at the Lowry Theatre. 'There were probably a few more trying to extricate themselves from Lowry Court the sheltered housing accommodation, ,' I joked.

The poems, sketches, short stories and reminiscences in this collection reaffirm the artist's place in Salford. They also bring to life lost moments such as the imagined conversation with the artist Valette and illuminate his ordinary life: I had no idea he was a regular at the Windmill pub! The whole work is a tribute to the passion and creativity of SWitCH writers. I had certainly learned much more about the place Lowry held in the hearts of people whom I represented, in the ward of Swinton North in which Lowry's Station Road home was located. I hope you enjoy reading through these stories as much as I have.

4

Acknowledgement

SWit'CH would like to thank The Lowry, Salford Quays for allowing us to reproduce some of the artist's works from what is the world's largest public collection of paintings and drawings by L S Lowry. Together, they reveal an artist who was a maverick: an artist who told his stories, his way. He spent much of his life here in Salford, and his work reflected the industrial landscape and the everyday lives of the people he saw around him. The collection goes much deeper, with Lowry's precise early sketchbook drawings, his remarkably empty seascapes, his compelling portraits and his surreal later sketches.

The exhibition, Modern Life: The LS Lowry Collection, features the works of L S Lowry both from The Lowry Collection and on loan from private lenders. The exhibition is displayed across four themed sections. *Our Lowry Sketchbook* includes pictures from each of these four sections:

Friends and Neighbours

City Lives

1887–1976: A Life of Drawing

Land and Sea.

Lowry said, "You don't need brains to be a painter, just feelings," and a similar sentiment could apply to our writers.

Lowry Galleries, Pier 8, The Quays, SALFORD, M50 3AZ.
Website:www.thelowry.com

A Portrait of Salford

Paul Hallows

The Lowry, Salford Quays

On 13th May 2025, me, my mum, Ruth, her cousin, and Terry, their friend, made our way to the Lowry Theatre, Salford Quays to attend the Lowry 360 exhibition. It was exciting and we were all looking forward to a unique experience. How unusual it would be to see Lowry's characters step out of the paintings and walk around.

We were taken into a dark room. Lowry's signature was on one of the walls, and on the right-hand side of the room was a portrait of one of Lowry's paintings: *Going to the Match*. It was all very atmospheric but I began to feel a bit disoriented. The ground felt strange – like a floating sensation.

The show then began. A woman's voice came over the speaker describing the paintings. An animated film was projected around the whole room. Everyone was quiet, watching, fascinated as the paintings came to life. A horse was trotting around, pulling a cart. From the painting *At the*

Match people walked around as others strolled amongst them as if we were meant to feel part of the football crowd. There was a lot of hustle and bustle.

The whole experience was like being inside one of his paintings: a touch of magic that helped me to feel transported back to the time of Lowry. As the characters moved it felt like we were moving along with them. It was both fascinating…and a little disturbing, partly because of the way we appeared to be moving about.

It was all a bit too much for Terry who is in his 80s. I sensed that he was feeling a bit anxious. Maybe it was bringing back his own memories of the time, taking him back to his childhood. Mum identified with it as well, being from Salford herself. It was interesting being able to go back and compare 'then' to now.

After the show, which was about fifteen minutes, we found a place in the cafe for Terry to sit down and relax.

Then we made our way into the gallery featuring Lowry's paintings of his 'matchstalk' men and dogs. Here were some I had never seen before: seascapes and pictures of Blackpool. I enjoyed looking at the seascapes, having visited Lytham and St. Anne's many times. They brought back memories of my own childhood, and I could imagine myself going for a swim in the sea that he had painted.

On the wall was a detailed time line of Lowry's life, starting from his birth in 1887 until he passed away in 1976, having lived to a great age. Each mentioned bits of information about his life in Swinton and Pendlebury. The time line mentioned about his time on Station Road, Swinton, and I thought how funny it was that my mum had also lived on Station Road.

Going to this exhibition has helped me to appreciate his paintings a lot more. Perhaps Lowry 360 will open minds and allow more people to fully appreciate and understand Lowry's unique style of art.

He Painted Life

Poem by Sylvia Edwards

He painted what he saw of life
In a northern town.
People hurrying to and fro,
Clad in black and brown.

He painted factory buildings,
Chimneys, belching smoke,
Grimy working places of,
Common Salford folk.

He painted cripples, bent on crutches
Men without their limbs.
The horror of the fever van,
Where life forever dims.

He painted terraced houses,
People in the street,
Church spire pointing to the sky,
Where life and death do meet.

He painted babies in their prams,
Crying children, dogs,
Soot-stained hovels, dark and grim,
Shrouded in their fog.

He painted war – a sad, blitzed site,
Bombed to rubble, waste,
Deadness, grey – no signs of life,
No more need for haste.

In simple lines and shapes he made,
His world breathe colour,
Drawings that help us imagine,
Courage and endeavour.

So, through oils, we understand,
This man who painted life,
In all its forms – its ups and downs,
Work, and toil and strife.

1958-4 COMING FROM THE MILL
© *The Lowry Collection, Salford*

Lowry's Signature

Sketch by Caroline Barden

Characters:

Alf – a guest at the hotel

Betty – Alf's wife

The scene:

The Seaburn Hotel, Sunderland.

3 a.m. in the morning on 2nd September 1968.

A twin-bedded guest room.

One bedside light is lit.

The door bangs open, and Alf and Betty enter the room. They are wearing their overcoats and shoes over their night clothes. They fall into each other s arms and Alf kicks the door shut with his foot.

ALF: Thank goodness that's over and we're both safe. Just our luck – a fire on our last night here!

BETTY: (*with a sob*) We could have been burnt alive! Never met our grandchildren! Then what would have happened?

Alf strokes Betty's hair.

BETTY: What a fright I got when the porter came hammering on our door. I didn't know what was happening or whether we'd get out in time.

ALF: Come on, Betty, don't take on. We're both alright and the fire's out now. Let's snuggle together in your bed and get warm.

Betty gently pushes away from Alf and gives herself a shake.

BETTY: Alright; but pass your coat over first. I'll hang them on these chairs to air. It might get rid of the smell of smoke.

She drapes the coats over the chairs and smooths down her nightie.

BETTY: I'm very glad I brought my winceyette. I must have had a premonition. Did you see that young woman who tripped up in the carpark? Poor thing, she landed really hard on her knees and then her babydoll went up round her armpits. Her husband was trying to cover her up with his pyjama top.

Alf sniggers.

ALF: I didn't know where to look!

BETTY: I'd have been mortified if that had happened to me. But she was more worried about her fluffy mules getting dirty than showing her bloomers. She made the ambulance man give her huge plasters so the blood from her grazes didn't get on them.

They both climb into a single bed together.

BETTY: I don't know whether I'll be able to get to sleep. If I close my eyes, I'll just see that black smoke again. And all that noise and clanging from the fire engines. It's put my nerves all on edge.

ALF: I counted five engines in the end. They must have sent some down from Newcastle, I suppose.

BETTY: That breathing apparatus the firemen put on was very bulky and heavy. And it made them look very strange. I'd have been terrified if they'd burst into my room looking like that.

ALF: A couple of people they brought out went straight into the ambulances. I hope they're going to be alright.

Betty shivers.

BETTY: Just think, that could have been us. What about that old artist? The one who's staying down our corridor. He was helped out by the manager, but perhaps he was just a bit shaky as he looked alright when he came with us to the annex room.

Betty gets out of bed. She pulls a folded napkin from her pocket.

ALF: Is that your hanky? I saw you waving it at the old man.

BETTY: No, it's a hotel napkin. And I didn't wave it at him! I went over to chat to him as he looked so lonely sitting all on his own with his cup of tea. But he didn't seem to want to chat, so in the end I just asked him to sign my napkin. He gave me a smile then. But after he'd signed it, he just turned away, so I left him to it.

ALF: Well, he might have felt a bit uncomfortable – it's the middle of the night and you're in your nightdress! What's his name?

BETTY: It's Mr Lowry. He does those pictures of matchstick men. He's quite famous. You must have seen his pictures in the newspapers.

ALF: Yes, maybe, I don't think I was very impressed. Perhaps he'll do one of us all running from the fire.

Betty hands Alf the napkin and gets back into bed. Alf holds it at arm's length with his finger and thumb.

ALF: It's just a dirty napkin – put it in the laundry.

BETTY: It's only got a splash of tea on it. And look, he's signed it nice and clearly. I'm going to keep it safe. It can be an heirloom for our grandchildren. It'll be worth something when Mr Lowry's dead. Imagine that!

ALF: Don't be so morbid!

BETTY: And I don't think he'll paint us in the carpark. He paints the seashore now – from his bedroom window apparently. I heard the waitresses talking about him at breakfast yesterday.

ALF: Eavesdropping again, were you?

BETTY: No!

Betty gives Alf a friendly punch.

BETTY: I heard one waitress say he'd offered to do a drawing for her, but she turned him down as she wasn't really interested in pictures. I wish he'd asked me – I'd have said yes! Anyway, no chance now. He'd have offered when I was chatting to him if he was going to.

ALF: Better get some sleep now. We've an early start in the morning for the train. I'm just off to the lav, then I'll get in my own bed.

Alf climbs out of bed and gives Betty a kiss. He leaves the room, and Betty folds the napkin carefully onto her bedside table. Then she lies down and pulls the covers up.

CURTAIN

'Going to the Match' – on Tour

Report by Chris Vickers

As well as his famous mill scenes and industrial landscapes, L S Lowry was also an avid football fan and Manchester City supporter. Though, for some reason his iconic picture *Going to the Match* was set at Bolton Wanderers ground, Burnden Park, in 1953, when they were a power in the land, losing to Blackpool in that season's legendary 'Matthews' FA Cup final.

Burnden Park's capacity was around 70,000 in those far off days when the majority of people worked five and a half day weeks and football acted as a release valve where they could vent their spleens regarding unjust refereeing decisions whilst being entertained by top players such as Tom Finney, Stanley Matthews and Raich Carter representing good teams.

The painting came about as Lowry entered a competition jointly sponsored by the Football Association and the newly formed Arts Council, where his picture was deemed the best of the 1700 efforts submitted. Interestingly Lowry said, "A street is not a street without people. The composition was incidental to the people." That, for me captures entirely the energy and passion of the crowd depicted in this scenario: fans scurrying to the match, wrapped up against chill winds, absorbed in the game ahead, determined to enjoy their spare time in the fervour and excitement of a big match.

It is the people who own the scene, and the enormous stadium in the background is, indeed, incidental. Unlike modern times, the games in those days kicked off at 3pm on Saturday afternoons to suit the mores of the day: work stopped at 12.30pm and kids' football games were played on Saturday mornings to allow attendance at the stadium. Oh!

And people walked to the ground and paid at the turnstiles on the day.

Going to the Match was owned by the Professional Football Association and had been on long term display at the Lowry Gallery for twenty-two years until they got into financial difficulties and decided to auction off the painting at Christies in October 2022. It could have disappeared into a private collection but was saved for the nation by a Lowry loving hedge-funder who donated £8.1 million towards its retention.

From the benefit of an Arts Council grant the painting 'played away' between 02/12/2023 and 01/02/2025, visiting Oldham, Blackpool, Birkenhead, Manchester's National Football Museum and Bury. There were workshops for both adults and children to hear about the great man, study the picture, and then, inevitably, have a go at painting their own versions of 'matchstick' men once so derided by sections of the population.

Lowry liked a bet when attending games and on one occasion, being hard up, offered up one of his pictures instead, to be told, "I've got a four-year-old who can paint better than that. I'll wait until you can pay me the shilling."

Collecting Rent from Mrs Grimes

Sketch by Bernie Shaw

Characters:

Mrs G – Mrs Grimes, a tenant

Mr G – Mr Grimes, Mrs Grimes's husband

Lowry – L S Lowry, rent collector and artist

Sloan – Mr Sloan, an artist.

Jones – Lowry's immediate superior, Mr Jones

Scene I

L S Lowry is on his rounds as a rent collector. He knocks on the door of the Grimes family; answered by Mrs Grimes, who looks ill.

Mrs G: Hello, Mr Lowry. I'm sorry, I haven't got this week's rent.

Lowry consults his book, Mrs Grimes pulls her shawl tighter.

Lowry: You didn't pay last week, either, Mrs Grimes.

Mrs G: My two children aren't well. They're both off school. And my man is off work. He's a docker. He's broke his leg.

Lowry: Eleven shillings, times two, is one pound, two shillings, Mrs Grimes. A large amount. My boss won't like it. Can't you get some help? Perhaps the relief fund at the Town Hall?

Mrs Grimes sniffs and shakes her head.

Mrs G: My husband's got some papers to fill in. But he's not very well educated.

The rough voice of Mrs Grimes's husband.

Mr G: Elsie, where's me dinner? I'm starving.

17

Lowry peeps in.

Lowry: Is that you, Mr Grimes? It's Mr Lowry here, the rent man.

Mr G: Rent! Rent! You can stick it, Mr Lowry. We're struggling. Like everyone else around here.

Lowry: It's no use getting angry, Mr Grimes. We have a problem.

More grumbling can be heard from Mr Grimes.

Lowry readdresses Mrs Grimes.

Lowry: I'll have to inform my superiors, Mrs Grimes. I'll see if I can do anything to help.

Scene II

Mr L S Lowry is a solitary man. Collecting rent in hard times, in hard areas, isn't easy. He is tall and large-framed. And the trilby hat he usually wears enhances his height. His size helps him: after all, he carries large amounts of money as he walks the lonely streets. Sometimes he goes inside his clients' homes. One time, a certain Mr Sloan tells Lowry that he is a painter. He invites Lowry in to see his paintings. Mr Lowry then invites Mr Sloan to come to his home in Pendlebury and view his own paintings.

Sloan: Mr Lowry, these paintings are wonderful. Just look at this dockside scene.

Lowry: Why…er, thank you.

Sloan: You've caught the atmosphere alright; those cranes and those dockers.

Lowry: Yes, but I have to do a lot of sketching first. You know, in my little pocketbook. Here, I'll show you.

Sloan: Well, however you do it, Mr Lowry, it seems to work. Tell you what, Mr Lowry, a fiver for this one?

18

Mr Sloan pulls out a big white five-pound note and waves it in the air. Mr Lowry is amazed, but declines, shaking his head. Incidents like this are rare – but the current situation with Mrs Grimes isn't. The dock land area where Lowry collects is tough; depravation and illness are common. It is on his mind as he catches the number 67 bus on Regent Road, back to his workplace in town.

Mr Jones, Lowry's immediate boss, is adamant.

Jones: No, Mr Lowry, this can't go on. Times are hard for everyone. If we let this Mrs Grimes woman continue like this, where would this firm be? So when you see her on Monday, tell her she has only two weeks to find the outstanding rent.

On the Monday morning, Mr Lowry is upset as he walks to Mrs Grimes's house. He knows he can't tell her what his boss has said. He knocks on her door. Mrs Grimes opens it. She looks just as ill as she was the week before, and ready to cry. But then, her mouth falls open, and her eyes widen at what Mr Lowry says.

Lowry: Mrs Grimes, my boss was not very kindly when I went to see him last week. But don't upset yourself as I've paid your rent for you.

Mrs G: Mr Lowry, I don't know what to say.

Lowry: I'm not rich, Mrs Grimes, but I am a single man and don't have troubles like you. If you pay next week's rent and give me a shilling a week extra, I'd be grateful.

Mrs G: It's me who should be grateful, Mr Lowry. Thank you, thank you. I'll do that, I promise.

Mrs Grimes grabs Mr Lowry's hand and squeezes it. Lowry smiles and tips his hat, then walks away. He has done this before. He knows how hard life is. He also understands his customers. Mrs Grimes will pay him back. He has studied the people he paints and knows more than anyone else that no matter how hard pressed, their integrity is sound.

L S Lowry Visiting Adolphe Valette

Rosemary Swift

Lowry: As you know, I have recently finished my time with you at your evening classes, Monsieur Valette. I have now enrolled for evening classes at Salford Art College which is conveniently near to where I work as a Rent Collector and closer to my family home in Swinton.

Valette: Well, keep up the good work, you show a lot of promise. As an admirer of Impressionism, I attempted to inspire my students likewise but now realise you must all find your own niche. I first came to Manchester to design greeting cards and calendars in 1905 and then I too enrolled as an evening student here at the Municipal School of Art. I was asked to join the staff as a teacher in 1907, so we have been acquaintances for nigh on ten years.

Lowry: Yes, I first came here as a student in 1905 when I lived in South Manchester which was more genteel to where I now dwell.

Valette: The scenes of Manchester inspired me when I came here and no doubt likewise the Salford backgrounds will have an influence on you.

Lowry: You will know of my new tutor, Bernard Taylor. He's an art critic for *The Manchester Guardian*. He tells me that my paintings are too murky and suggests I paint my canvases a flaky white. My father – who would have liked to dabble in art – is fascinated by this idea.

Valette: As I've said, you must develop your own style.

Lowry: I am grateful for your early influence of Impressionism which I reflected in my earlier works, but at the moment I am beginning to visualise crowd scenes needing to be depicted as sticklike figures against the said white background. Your oil painting of a bent-over chap pushing a cart in Albert Square, Manchester is an inspiration.

Valette: For too long, art has reflected what is enjoyable for the upper classes. We are presently in the midst of a World War and do not know its effects once it is over. Soon, God willing.

Lowry: I am grateful not having to serve due to flat feet. I can continue with my art work.

Valette: You have been given a good opportunity as opposed to many of your former colleagues. Be true to yourself – paint what you see and what you want to paint. Good luck for your future. Well, I'll say goodbye to you now.

1952-3 - View from Window of Royal Tech College, Salford, towards Manchester 1924

Supper in the Windmill

Lorraine Tattersall

Every Saturday night, off he would go from his house on Station Road, Swinton, in his long Macintosh and trilby hat, his notepad and pencil tucked in his inside pocket, no mobile phones back then, and make his way to the Windmill Pub where he would sit quietly in a corner with his one drink of the night, either a sherry, or half of Sam's best bitter, notepad and pencil laid beside ready for him to pick up and draw the regular characters that frequented this hostelry.

Also on a Saturday night, a couple called Dennis and Evelyn made their way to the Windmill where they both worked, Dennis as a bar tender and Evelyn, the sandwich maker, then when all her sandwiches were out ready for the Saturday night rush she became the pot collector.

Her speciality was roast ham sandwiches, whist pork pies, that Dennis said were the best in Pendlebury, and a bowl of lip-smacking Norco pickles delivered fresh from their factory which was just across the road from the pub.

As the Windmill got busier by the hour, nobody took much notice of Mr Mac (the nickname the customers called him, as no one knew much about him). He kept himself to himself, quite happy in his own company, and only spoke when he tipped his hat to bid them all goodnight when he was leaving.

Evelyn felt sorry for him and told Dennis that she was going to speak to him the next time he came in. So the following Saturday, Dennis served him with his choice of drink, and Evelyn went over to offer him a sandwich, whist pie and a plate of pickles which he gladly accepted as he had not eaten since lunch time, and through this good gesture, a Saturday night friendship was formed.

One Saturday when Evelyn was clearing a table, Mr Mac asked her if he could have the empty cigarette box the customer had left. She gave it to him and watched as he gently opened it, laid it flat, then picked up his pencil and began to draw. Evelyn took the empties to the bar and went to clear another table, then on her way back Mr Mac handed her the little sketch he had done on the cigarette packet.

"Oh thank you very much," she said, taking it over to show Dennis who replied, "very nice" with a frown, propping it up at the side of the till, where it stayed for a while.

The following week when Mr Mac came in, Evelyn took over his plate of food and also a blank sheet of paper asking him if he wouldn't mind drawing her a picture, one she could frame to remember him by, as he had told her the week before that he would be leaving Pendlebury in a couple of weeks. He took the paper and said it would be a pleasure and told her how he would miss the pub and most of all her suppers.

When the next Saturday night came, Mr Mac gave Evelyn the drawing he had promised. She didn't know what to make of it as she had never seen the like of it before, but thanked him and kissed him on the cheek. He flushed, then raised his glass saying "cheers" as he downed the last of his half pint in the Windmill, then left.

On the way home Evelyn said to Dennis, "I'm going to frame this picture and hang it in the hall, because it's ever so unusual, and you never know, Mr Mac might be a famous artist one day."

"Frame it, I don't think so," was Dennis's reply.

"Who would want to buy a drawing of some drab stick-looking gloomy figures huddled around a bar? Why our little Jimmy could do better than that, and he's only six."

Sadly the drawing never got framed and was put in a drawer, and over the years must have got thrown away when Evelyn was having a clear out.

24

Then many, many years later when they were both watching the television, it came on the news that a painting had been sold for millions of pounds at Christie's in London.

Evelyn turned to Dennis and said, "Oh Dennis, look at that, I should have kept that drawing Mr Mac did for me all those years ago. We could have been sitting on a fortune all this time. I can still see it clearly now, of those funny looking stick people in the Windmill, and he signed it too,. That in itself could have brought us a few bob. It said:

"With Love to Evelyn, from L S Lowry 1948."

1961-20 - GENTLEMAN LOOKING AT SOMETHING 1960

© The Lowry Collection, Salford

A Brief Encounter

Colin Balmer

Janet's first speed dating evening had been an interesting experience. Most of the interviews were never going to progress beyond the sampler. The quadruple divorces, the histories of gaol, the extolled virtues of alcohol and serial cohabiting were all outside the experiences she wanted to share. But John at fifty-four was charming, well-dressed and well-spoken but especially interested in her. They exchanged basic life-style details. She, forty-eight and widowed, had extended her erstwhile hobby to become a fine art dealer with her own collection of rare prints by contemporary artists like Warhol, Hurst, Hockney and, her special passion, L S Lowry. John was "something in the city" and now liberated after a lifetime caring for his recently deceased mother. He had, she discovered, studied fine art for an Open University masters and therefore could engage emotionally on that level with Janet. She liked his sensitivity for their shared passion; and she virtually tingled with excitement when he praised her commitment to art.

But, eternally careful, she was not going to be drawn in by any seductive, "Come up and see my etchings," bait. On the contrary, she made the first invitation.

"You must come to my Quays apartment and I'll show you the pictures I have retained in my own collection as well as those in my catalogue."

"That would be nice. I was going to suggest we have a look round Manchester Art Gallery together this weekend. Maybe I'll take you up on your offer some time when we know each other better."

They enjoyed their Saturday, with The Old Master in the gallery followed by a trip down Oxford Road to soak up the delights of the watercolour collection in the Whitworth. They exchanged opinions and feelings on common intellectual grounds. She was delighted by his interest in her Lowry collection in particular.

"Which is your favourite? Why the specific interest in Lowry?"

"Samuel, my late husband, was a self-made successful business man, born and bred in Salford. He started the collection and it's my beautiful memory of our twelve years together. I'd hate to lose them; Hockney, Hurst and Warhol could go on a bonfire first."

"I bet they are pretty valuable then?" he suggested.

As they surveyed the pictures in the galleries, he had her enthralled as their interchange moved from brooding analysis of sombre biblical executions through to explosively brilliant sunflowers, through comical satire – and what about those Turner skies? Any reserve she had felt about meeting a new companion evaporated as they talked about application by the masters of cobalt blue, cadmium yellow and titanium white. They contrasted these exuberant hues with Lowry's limited palette of flake white, ivory black, vermilion, Prussian blue and yellow ochre. Never in the last six years had she felt so comfortable and relaxed. She felt the grip of his grief was also being loosened. It was the unavoidable consequence of this empathy that the invitation to her apartment was offered again and promptly accepted the same evening.

In the morning her life changed as she studied the bare walls.

Men in Caps – or Bowler Hats

Poem by Bob Farrell

1941-8 COMING FROM THE MILL
© *The Lowry Collection, Salford*

I'm just reading about L S Lowry.
An artist of great renown.
Whose simple childish paintings
Are now selling for thousands of pounds.

Next February is the fiftieth anniversary of his death,
And for that I'm researching the man.
I'm starting from when he lived in Pendlebury,
Which is the time his style of painting began.

For a living he collected rents around Salford.
He did this for over forty years, for the same firm.
Caught the train to Manchester every morning to their offices.
Then home to Pendlebury and his mother he'd return.

After missing his train one winter morning,
With a half hour wait before the next was due,
He stood and looked across at a local mill,
To the gateway where workers passed through.

Men in caps or bowler hats were entering together.
Some veered to the left, others to the right.
Lowry knew the caps did the heavy manual work,
And the bowler hat pen pushers did the light.

On the train into Manchester, he got to thinking,
Of how he would capture on canvas the scene,
Of those millworkers leaving after their day's toil.
It was the dawning of his matchstick-men theme.

Undaunted, Lowry presented his ideas on canvas.
He would observe normal people – adapt in his mind's eye,
His concept – that realistic shape and form are unnecessary,
And that realism can be forfeited to apply.

Lowry painted women, children and animals.
Recognisable, but disjointed, for a better word.
He drew streets and parks and a football ground.
In all honesty, some scenes were absurd.

Lowry's mother, Elizabeth, was uncomplimentary,
Of this simplistic style he had ventured upon.
Her miserable life and her own failed ambitions,
Led to a sarcastic diatribe of comments to her son.

Most Salford folk had heard the name Lowry,
Then Brian and Michael's song enhanced his fame.
But was it *his* creations that helped sell their record?
Or was it *they* who gave Lowry more acclaim?

Lowry would fill his canvases with crowds of people,
Amidst local areas many of us would recognise.
Smoking chimneys on our houses and factories,
Yet he would also paint seashores against cloudy skies.

For 70 years Lowry produced hundreds of paintings,
But only a small percentage ever saw the light of day.
His quick sketches were distributed to every Tom, Dick and
Harriet.
His cleaning lady used to throw them away.

Lowry listened to his critics with temerity.
His kind of impressionism was open to critique.
Eyebrows were raised by art professionals and laymen.
But this man was a first and a first is always unique.

So much more can be said about Lowry,
But I've concentrated on his Pendlebury days.
They were his first steps towards artistic notoriety.
So, L S Lowry, you deserve your bouquets.

Matchstalk Man

Sketch by Bernie Shaw

Characters:

Mrs G – Mrs Grimes, a tenant

LSL – L S Lowry, rent-collector and artist

Joan and Elsie – neighbours

Willis – Mr Willis, a man with his leg in plaster

Mother – L S Lowry's mother, bedbound

Sylvia – an art student

Scene I

(A back street, gas-o-meter back drop. Two girls – one skipping, both singing. Three women and a man look on.)

Girls: He's a collier from Pendlebury Brew…brew… brew.

    He can push a wagon up a brew…brew…brew. When he gets to the top, he can

(a cheeky young boy runs in on stage and joins in)

    have a bottle of pop. He's a collier from Pendlebury Brew.

Mrs G: Bugger off, Billy Smith. Don't come round here spoiling the girls' games. *(Boy pulls a funny face)* Oh, that's nice, that is. You don't even live in this street.

Boy: *(pulls a bigger face)* Shut it, missus!

Mrs G: Yer cheeky little sod! I know yer mam. She works at Woolies on Regent Road. Toy counter. I'll see her later.

(The boy runs off. Girls too. Lowry enters. Two women at front doors chatting. Man sits opposite, plastered leg up on chair. Mrs Grimes sits front stage right.)

LSL: *(tips trilby hat)* Afternoon, Mrs Grimes.

Mrs G: Afternoon, Mr Lowry. Got it right here. *(looks over at two women)* Ten bob rent.

LSL: Very good, Mrs Grimes.

Mrs G: Haven't missed in six years. *(looks over again at two women)* More than I can say for some as lives round here. Them as likes a big "carry out" jug o' beer.

LSL: Now, now, Mrs Grimes.

Mrs G: The church and law. Me. Methodist, and proud of it, Mr Lowry.

LSL: Yes, Mrs Grimes. No need for all that. We're all different, with different circumstances.

Mrs G: Aye, that's as may be. But me? I like to watch the kids playing.

LSL: Me too! Captivating! Spindly though, these days, don't you think.

Mrs G: Government that! Rickets! And parents struggling.

LSL: They're feisty though. See the camaraderie in crowds. All bending together against the wind.

Mrs G: Against oppression, more like. Bloody government!

LSL: *(smiles)* Could be.

Mrs G: Still sketching, Mr Lowry?

LSL: Oh, yes. Down the Adelphi, later. Good day to you, Mrs G. *(walks over to the two women)* Hello ladies *(tips his hat)*.

Elsie:	Sorry, Mr Lowry. Can we pay next week? My fella's off sick. Docker!
Joan:	Mine too. Hard times.
LSL:	I'll mark it down so.
Joan:	Yes, you do that, Mr Lowry.
LSL:	Try and find it for next week though. The Pall Mall Company, my bosses, won't like it.
Joan:	Sod 'em, Mr Lowry.
Elsie:	Yeah. What do they know?
Joan:	Not Salford's famous number nine dock. That's for sure.
Elsie:	Amen to that!
Joan:	And what's she, Mrs Perfect over there, been saying?
Elsie:	Bet she never misses a bloody payment.
Joan:	Presbyterian! Did she give you all that religious malarkey?
Elsie:	Yeah! Upholder of the law? While her old man's out breaking in. Working late (*laughs*).
Joan:	Very late, if you know what we mean?
Elsie:	Very dark. Very black. When all the shops are shut.

(*Elsie and Joan both laugh.*)

LSL:	(*tips his hat*) Ladies…Mrs Grimes? Methodist, actually! (*walks away*).

(*LSL stops. Talks to Mr Willis, plaster-cast man.*).

LSL:	Hello, Mr Willis. How's the leg. Mind if I sketch you?
Willis:	Not going to cost me, is it?
LSL:	No. not this time. (*laughs*) The leg?

Willis:	Itchy. Plaster's coming off next week. Don't know when I'm back at work though.
LSL:	(*sketching*) Salford Docks, isn't it? The big crane?
Willis:	Yes.
LSL:	Scary?
Willis:	In the wind it is. Bloody high.
LSL:	I bet.
Willis:	I liked those sketches you did last week. Very good, Mr Lowry.
LSL:	The Ancoats ones?
Willis:	And the dosshouse.
LSL:	Park St. lodgings, Cross Lane?
Willis:	Still the dosshouse round here.
LSL:	Life's unfortunates.
Willis:	Do you sell many paintings, Mr Lowry?
LSL:	Not really. My subject matter isn't that appealing. Or so I'm told.
Willis:	Shame. They're very good. Someday, Mr Lowry. Someday.
LSL:	Thank you, Mr Willis. Thank you. (*tips hat, walks away*).

EXIT

Scene II

(*Bedroom. 117, Station Road, Swinton. Late evening.*)

Mother:	(*banging on the floor*) Laurie? Laurie? Laurence Lowry? Where is that silly son of mine? Laurence…? (*Lowry enters*)

35

LSL:	I'm here, Mother. It's alright. I'm here.
Mother:	About time.
LSL:	I've brought you some tea and biscuits.
Mother:	Tea? Biscuits? As if that will change the world. A world gone mad!
LSL:	There, there, Mother. Don't go on. The world will take care of itself.
Mother:	Says you, Laurence. Says you!
LSL:	Let's chat, Mother. How's your day been?
Mother:	How do you think it's been? Stuck in here. Every day.
LSL:	You could get up, Mother. Walk around a bit. Listen to the wireless.
Mother:	Wireless? Nothing but rubbish. Did you do what I asked you to?
LSL:	What was that, Mother?
Mother:	What a memory. The bank! I asked you to go to the bank. Get me a statement.
LSL:	Sorry, Mother. I'll go in tomorrow. I forget sometimes.
Mother:	Forget your head, if it was loose.
LSL:	I've been working on some paintings.
Mother:	Paintings? Call them paintings? Those funny squiggly daubings. Those aren't paintings. Not real paintings.
LSL:	I enjoy them, Mother. It's something a bit different.
Mother:	(*nastily*) They're different alright. Pah! Now Matisse, Michelangelo, Turner and Van Gogh…well. They're real painters. The world knows and admires them.

LSL:	Quite right too, Mother. But different styles. Different era.
Mother:	Talent is talent, Laurence. Paintings by these artists hang in galleries all over the world.
LSL:	True, Mother. And good for them. Lights unto the world.
Mother:	What?
LSL:	Dedication. They're all dedicated artists. Like me.
Mother:	Like you? You'll never understand. You're putting yourself alongside artists like them?
LSL:	Well...er...no, Mother, but...
Mother:	Money, Laurence! Look at us. Your father, Robert, died years ago. Leaving debts. Now, here we are. Station Road, Swinton.
LSL:	It's alright, Mother.
Mother:	It's not alright! In Stretford we had standing.
LSL:	Standing?
Mother:	Yes! And in Victoria Park, Rusholme, we had respect. We've gone down. Haven't you noticed? Station Road. (*derisively*) Station bloody Road!
LSL:	I like it, Mother. Not at first. But now it's alright.
Mother:	(*shakes head)* What an assumption.
LSL:	Lots of characters scurrying about round windy corners. All hell bent on something or other.
Mother:	Lords and ladies, are they? Don't think so.
LSL:	I like them, Mother. They are friendly. Going around Salford tomorrow. Going sketching. Hodge Lane.
Mother:	(*horrified)* Hodge Lane? See what I mean?
LSL:	Hodge Lane Wash-house, actually.

37

Mother:	*(shakes head)* The idea!
LSL:	Lots of women. Pushing prams along with big bundles of washing in them.
Mother:	It's not Park Lane, London, is it?
LSL:	Wouldn't want it to be, Mother.
Mother:	Laurie…I give up.
LSL:	Practise your piano. You like that.
Mother:	To play for whom? People around here?
LSL:	For yourself, Mother. Good for your soul.
Mother:	You worry about your own soul. You're so annoying, sometimes.
LSL:	*(sheepishly)* Sorry, Mother. Goodnight.

EXIT

Scene III

LSL: *(Still in his mother's room. She is now dead. He is now sat looking at her picture.)* Still can't believe it, Mother. It's nearly a year now. I'm still all alone. "A funny turn," you said, Mother. You recovered, then two days later you were gone. Remember when I looked out of the window and described the scene: it was very windy. You laughed about the roly-poly man running after his cap. It rolled like a wheel in the gutter. *(LSL laughs)* A cat chased it too. The man kicked it up the backside. *(laughs again)*. Bloody cats. And dogs. I can never draw 'em. They come out all smudgy. *(He gets up, ambles around the room)* What a life, Mother. *(He picks up her hairbrush, smiles…to the audience)* She was beautiful, my mother, to me at least. Buried at Southern Cemetery. Frustrated dreams. Sad! You were good on the piano, Mother. Loved hearing you

38

play. Concert standard you were. Your illness? Your bed was a refuge, I reckon. But I did like our late-night chats. (*reflective*) What's it all about? You were always a bit snooty, Mother. Swinton's not so bad. There's worse places. I'm glad you missed this terrible war. Bad news coming out of Europe....

This Hitler fella seems crazy! He's gunning for Jewish people. What's that all about? The Cohens down Regent Rd, in Salford, are always nice to me. Always get a cup of tea from them when I'm there. I collect in some Jewish areas. Right there, in Salford. Oh, and Regent Rd and Cross Lane. They're okay! No problems. (*pulls scraps of paper out of pockets*) Here's Cross Lane. Two drunks. (*chuckles*) Trying to thump each other. Did this last week. Plenty of action around these. The markets just nearby. A lot of colourful characters there too! Some fellas juggle plates on make-shift stages. Marvellous really! I'll try sketching there one day. Well, Mother, I need to work now. So, till next time...love you. Glad you missed this war. Got rationing now. Pain in the you know what!

Scene IV

(Scene: artists, classrooms, easels, pupils)

LSL: (*pointing*) The perspective is good, Sylvia.

Sylvia: Thanks, Mr Lowry. Maddening though. Can't always get it.

LSL: Of course it is, my dear. That's what keeps us all going...and excited.

Sylvia: And the vanishing points...frustrating.

39

LSL:	Stick at it. (*laughs*) My vanishing point vanished years ago. Forever! My silly little paintings.
Sylvia:	Silly, Mr Lowry? Wouldn't say that. You're getting quite a name for yourself. I've seen your paintings in Salford Art Gallery. And in magazines and papers. Your 'match-like' figures are brilliant.
LSL:	(*chuckles*) Match-like? Just newspaper talk. Art is very personal. We all see objects and people differently. The big boys said I was just a Sunday painter! Posh papers. Sickening!
Sylvia:	They did? What did you say?
LSL:	I said, yes, a Sunday painter, every day of the week.
Sylvia:	Good for you. And I've heard about your little stories.
LSL:	Stories?
Sylvia:	Figures of your own imagination?
LSL:	My own little world. Special visions. The real world can be frightening.
Sylvia:	Scary alright. You worked so hard. How did you find the time to paint?
LSL:	Late at night. When my mother was alive, I'd attend to her about ten o'clock.
Sylvia:	Commendable, Mr Lowry.
LSL:	Then I'd go and paint 'till about two in the morning. Later still, sometimes. No brains. Only feelings!
Sylvia:	Goodness me. Not many do that. Now you're here, teaching in Manchester Art School?
LSL:	And Salford Tech. My mother died in '39. Glad she missed the war years.

Sylvia: A kind of blessed relief.

LSL: I then had more time to paint. My father had died in 1932. So it was all down to me. You staying late, Sylvia?

Sylvia: Just for a bit, Mr Lowry. Sixish.

LSL: How is the art going? Paintings okay?

Sylvia: Fine thanks. But it's just one of my hobbies actually.

LSL: Oh, what other things do you do?

Sylvia: Dancing, swimming, tennis.

LSL: My, you are busy.

Sylvia: I like my art, but you, Mr Lowry, it's your life.

LSL: You're right. Compulsive. I'm happiest with a pencil and paper to sketch with.

Sylvia: That's marvellous, and it shows.

LSL: Thank you. (*still sketching*) Never a sports person like you.

Sylvia: Never?

LSL: Well, when I was growing up there weren't any sports clubs like there are now. But I do like football.

Sylvia: Which team?

LSL: Manchester City. The Blues. I try to get to Maine Road a lot.

Sylvia: What about the Reds?

LSL: Nothing against Manchester United. Working class heroes, like City. It's parochial is football. You support your local team. I was born in Stretford but spent some years in Rusholme as a kid, so I followed City. Nearest team.

41

Sylvia:	I see.
LSL:	Course, if you lived in Salford where I collected some rents, you'd support the Reds. Lots of United fans there.
Sylvia:	I know. I've seen it down Trafford Road on Saturdays.
LSL:	(*laughs*) Packed, eh? Crowds streaming over Trafford Bridge?
Sylvia:	Murder, if you're trying to catch a bus.
LSL:	And it's those excited fans I try to sketch.
Sylvia:	Didn't you paint a football picture?
LSL:	Yes. Two in fact. *Saturday Afternoon* and *A Football Match*. It sold for more than five thousand pounds.
Sylvia:	That's a massive amount of money.
LSL:	I go into some of those fans' houses. They're hard-working people. And not a lot to show for it.
Sylvia:	Friendly people though.
LSL:	Yes, but I've seen other types. Fights and that.
Sylvia:	I've got a friend down near the docks. Mostly skint but she'd give you anything.
LSL:	It's that hardship I try to capture.
Sylvia:	Never thought of that.
LSL:	You'll never see happy, smiling faces in my works.
Sylvia:	Sad!
LSL:	I've been fortunate. Left school just after my fourteenth birthday and stepped into my job as a rent collector.
Sylvia:	Good for you, Mr Lowry.

LSL:	Did it all my life.
Sylvia:	(*asks to see sketch*) May I take a peek?
LSL:	Oh, it's not much.
Sylvia:	(*gets up*) Oh, it's really good! And there's some other bits in the corners.
LSL:	Just some characters I saw yesterday in Ancoats. Couple of drunks actually.
Sylvia:	You must see some sights on your travels.
LSL:	Lots. Some good. Some not so good. My regular job was easy compared to other people's.
Sylvia:	A great deal of walking?
LSL:	Kept me fit. If I'd worked on the docks or in a grim factory, I might not have been an artist.
Sylvia:	Good point.
LSL:	I was getting paid to walk and mingle with my characters. And study scenes and factories. They became my artistic works.
Sylvia:	Very colourful, Mr Lowry.
LSL:	Northern scenes. On parade. Just for me.
Sylvia:	Romantic, don't you think?
LSL:	It's all very well being 'arty' but if I had a wife and a couple of kids to think about, things might've been different.
Sylvia:	Did you think about other painters? Their fame? Struggles?
LSL:	Quite a lot actually.
Sylvia:	Like who?
LSL:	Of all the great artists, my favourite is Dante Rossetti. He painted women really well.

Sylvia:	Women? What about the great Leonardo Da Vinci? *Mona Lisa*?
LSL:	A masterpiece indeed! But that work of art is a head. It's not the whole woman. It hangs, of course, in the Louvre, Paris.
Sylvia:	I know. Have you seen it?
LSL:	Only in graphic form. Magazines. Newspapers.
Sylvia:	That smile.
LSL:	World famous! No eyebrows. Did you know that?
Sylvia:	What? Didn't know that.
LSL:	Maybe that helped the smile. Artistic trick. Genius, Da Vinci. What style! Magic.
Sylvia:	How did you get your style, Mr Lowry?
LSL:	Who knows? I always tried to paint real life. The stark North. Intriguing!
Sylvia:	That does come out. What started it?
LSL:	A missed train.
Sylvia:	Really?
LSL:	Pendlebury Railway Station. The Acme building just nearby.
Sylvia:	And that was it?
LSL:	It was the whole scene. Twilight was just coming in. There were lots of windows. They glowed yellow from the lights inside. Stood out in the gloom. Fascinating.
Sylvia:	And your colours? What paints do you use?
LSL:	Only about four, or five. Blues, yellows and that. I like using black and white too. Any more would detract.

Sylvia:	To be self-taught, and paint like you do… (*LSL interrupts her*)
LSL:	Not entirely self-taught. A lot of people think that. I studied under a wonderful impressionist, named Adolphe Vallette.
Sylvia:	Wonderful, Mr Lowry. Lucky you.
LSL:	And a posh place in London exhibited my work, just before the war.
Sylvia:	Really? Which one?
LSL:	Lefeure Gallery. 1939. That was nice for me.
Sylvia:	You had fire in your belly. Good days, eh?
LSL:	Again, I was fortunate. When I was seventeen or so, Paris was the place for artists.
Sylvia:	Ah, yes. We all know about Paris.
LSL:	Picasso and his 'gang', as I like to call 'em, scrabbled about in dingy rooms and cellars. You know, around Montmartre.
Sylvia:	You make everything sound funny. And interesting.
LSL:	They were all young 'chancers', those would-be artists. Very few had a regular job like mine.
Sylvia:	You were working hard then, Mr Lowry.
LSL:	I was, it's true. Regular job! But I often wonder about that.
Sylvia:	How do you mean?
LSL:	Well, if Picasso and his mates had worked in proper jobs, we might not have their master pieces now!
Sylvia:	That's an interesting point.
LSL:	Incidentally, the world-famous artist, Van Gogh, never sold a painting. Did you know that?

Sylvia:	I'm amazed. His paintings now sell for hundreds of thousands of pounds.
LSL:	His brother did give him some money for a painting. Just so Van Gogh could buy some brushes.
Sylvia:	Hard to comprehend.
LSL:	Picasso struggled too. Which artist didn't in Paris of the early 1900s?
Sylvia:	No justice. World's mad!
LSL:	Picasso had rolled-up canvases, future masterpieces in a wheelbarrow. He'd flit around the back streets of Paris with them. Dodging debtors.
Sylvia:	How on earth did they all get by?
LSL:	(*laughs*) Drink! The wine probably helped! But desire prevailed. Desire to create art.
Sylvia:	Desire?
LSL:	To paint was everything! Me? Yes, I had desire. But I also had a steady, regular job.
Sylvia:	Constant conflict. Must've been hard.
LSL:	Maybe I was a coward? Snail-like aspirations.
Sylvia:	Don't say that, Mr Lowry. You had commitments. And you stuck to them. Your mother and father. Maybe Picasso and his mates were cowards?
LSL:	If he was, I'm glad. Imagine a world without his, and his gang's, beautiful works of art. I'm glad they all emerged.
Sylvia:	You emerged too. And on the world's stage, Mr Lowry. Put the industrial landscape on the map.
LSL:	(*chuckles*) My own little school of art, eh? The 'Northerner'!

Sylvia:	Certainly! And there's nothing wrong with that.
LSL:	(*pauses sketching*) You know, I do go to other places. And paint there.
Sylvia:	Where, exactly?
LSL:	I love the sea. And I love doing seascapes.
Sylvia:	Me too! Blackpool. Frothy waves and that.
LSL:	Menacing waves too, sometimes. Powerful forces, rushing onwards. Straight towards you.
Sylvia:	Never seen it like that.
LSL:	The North Sea can be wild. I like Sunderland, in the North East.
Sylvia:	Oh, I've been there.
LSL:	Solid, working-class people. I stay in Seaburn, usually.
Sylvia:	I've been nearby, in Whitburn.
LSL:	I know Whitburn. A bit posher. Not as gritty. Bigger houses. (*laughs*) And pay packets.
Sylvia:	Did you sketch up there?
LSL:	A bit. Abandoned rowing boats. Seascapes. Mostly I was resting.
Sylvia:	You deserved a rest.
LSL:	Couldn't wait to get back though. Smoky stacks. Cobbled streets. Terraced houses. People. Factories.
Sylvia:	North West, steeped in your soul. Did the war years affect you?
LSL:	Not really. Too old for combat. So I wasn't called up.
Sylvia:	Yes, of course.

LSL:	But I did want to help, so I volunteered to be a fire-watcher.
Sylvia:	How did you manage that? You had work to do.
LSL:	Glad to do it. A couple of nights a week I was on top of Lewis's store on Market St.
Sylvia:	Good for you. Creepy at night?
LSL:	No, I could look all over Piccadilly and the gardens. Sketch central Manchester.
Sylvia:	Well done, Mr Lowry.
LSL:	Nothing stopped me sketching.
Sylvia:	Non-stop. A drawing machine.
LSL:	In the late forties my works started to sell.
Sylvia:	I read that somewhere.
LSL:	Do you know Daisy Nook?
Sylvia:	Rochdale way, isn't it?
LSL:	Sort of. Lovely wooded area. Big fair every year. Painted it. People seemed to like it. I did too.
Sylvia:	Any other people in your life, Mr Lowry?
LSL:	No. It's just me and my cat. And I'm retiring soon.
Sylvia:	You, retiring. Not from painting, surely?
LSL:	Never! Not from painting. Silly squiggles or not!
Sylvia:	Thought so. Rent collecting, yes. More time for your art, eh?
LSL:	That's it.
Sylvia:	(*looks at watch*) I'd better be going. It's nearly six. I'm meeting a friend in Piccadilly. See you next week. (*she goes*)
LSL:	'Night, Sylvia.

EXIT

48

Scene V

(Same street as at beginning of play.)

LSL: Hello, Mrs Grimes. How are you?

Mrs G: (*sat by door*) Oh, hello, Mr Lowry. Mondayish. We all get older, eh? (*rubs her legs*)

LSL: Indeed we do. Bones creak!

Mrs G: Me rheumatics are giving me some gyp lately.

LSL: Sorry to hear that, Mrs Grimes. I've called to tell you that I'm retiring soon. You might get a new collector next week.

Mrs G: Aw, Mr Lowry. Never saw you retiring.

LSL: Comes to us all. And I've moved to Mottram in Cheshire.

Mrs G: Ooh, nice. Very posh. Like it?

LSL: Not much. Prefer being in the city. And these little back streets. They intrigue me.

Mrs G: Gerroff with yer. Been trying to get away from here for years. Retiring? You'll never retire from painting. It's in yer blood!

LSL: Why, thank you, Missus Grimes.

Mrs G: You're famous! Round here, at least. You're 'Matchstalk Man'.

LSL: Am I? Really? Funny, that.

Mrs G: Yes. Yer little figures are great. Seen 'em in Salford Art Gallery. Peel Park.

LSL: Good. That's really nice they have put them in there. My paintings? Displayed!

Mrs G: What do you mean, good? Proud to have them, I should think.

LSL: Thank you, Mrs Grimes.

Mrs G: You know what, Mr Lowry.

LSL: What?

Mrs G: We all have to pass on. But I think your paintings will last forever!

LSL: (*touched*) Thank you so much. And you know what, Mrs Grimes? (*winks*) So do I…so do I. (*turns, walks off*)

Scene VI

(*Same street. Dark. Moody lighting. Single streetlamp. Houses gone. Wasteland.*)

LSL: (*plaintive, philosophical*) Is this it? All there is? Life? A wasteland? Those streets? Those houses? Those people? All gone? People who just wouldn't lie down. Adversity constant. And I, collecting rent, so they might stay, one more day…to dream? (*dabs eyes*)

(*A man approaches. Silhouette*)

Willis: Mr Lowry? My word, is it really you? Back here? Are you alright?

LSL: Mr Willis (*surprised*). How extraordinary!

Willis: You crying, Mr Lowry?

LSL: Oh…er, no (*dabs eyes*). Just this late-night autumn breeze. Soon winter winds will be blowing in.

Willis: That they will, Mr Lowry. Saw you on television last week.

LSL: Was it good? You enjoy it?

Willis: Very good. And interesting.

LSL: Ah, television.

Willis:	We've had two new collectors since you left, Mr Lowry. Who'd have thought? Our Mr Lowry, famous?
LSL:	Oh, I don't know. I've been lucky.
Willis:	Hard work lucky.
LSL:	You know, Mr Willis, it's like there's a big silver ball bouncing over the hills, valleys and crowded city streets.
Willis:	How do you mean, Mr Lowry?
LSL:	No matter how hard you try, you can't ever catch it. The ball's always out of reach. Dreamlike…you reach out, uselessly.
Willis:	Is that so?
LSL:	Elusive! Like life. And then time itself. Gone. Forever!
Willis:	Don't feel down, Mr Lowry. You proved your ideas, and style, were right. No-one paints like you.
LSL:	No-one paints like me (*muses*). How kind, Mr Willis. I wish my mother and father could hear that. I hope I caught it all. Landscapes. People. Hardship.
Willis:	You did, Mr Lowry. You did.
LSL:	Can I tell you a secret?
Willis:	Certainly, Mr Lowry.
LSL:	They wanted to honour me.
Willis:	Who did, Mr Lowry?
LSL:	The Queen, and her officials, I suppose.
Willis:	(*eyes wide*) The Queen?

LSL: The offices of her Majesty, anyway. Well, I turned them all down. Told Harold Wilson, PM, and Edward Heath!

Willis: (*astonished*) Really? Why?

LSL: I've asked myself that same question. They were kind to ask. Various titles…gongs? But…hmm…somehow, I… OBE. CBE?

Willis: For heaven's sake! Your paintings now hang in some world-famous places.

LSL: I've worked in too many hard-bitten places and areas. Fancy baubles…not sure?

Willis: I'm sorry to hear that, Mr Lowry.

LSL: I wasn't quite sure which side I was on…what was it you said? No-one paints like you? Now I know. Thanks again, Mr Willis. "No-one paints like you". I'll settle just for that.

(Tips his hat. Walks off. Mr Willis stands and stares.)

EXIT

(As Lowry walks off, the song, 'Dirty Old Town' is playing.)

L S Lowry: An Unlikely Genius?

Eric Lowndes

We were a young married couple with small children, and we needed a new picture to hang above the fireplace in the living room. We wanted something that was both interesting and inexpensive. Our first picture had been of a knight, a lady and a dragon that we had bought from the local shop. I remember it with fondness. The kids had loved it. The reds and black had complemented the living coal fire and the subdued evening lighting perfectly. We had reluctantly skipped the painting because its corners had suffered a few nicks and scratches, and its surrounding border had become scruffy. The kids were sad to see it go. It had served us and their imaginations well.

The painting we chose as its replacement was a complete contrast. It was an L S Lowry Manchester mill scene. What had attracted me to it was its unusual style, its inexpensive price, and that it was the perfect size to fit over our fireplace. It was an industrial landscape, apparently signed by Lowry. As time passed, the picture moved with us to new homes and somehow, somewhere, along with the years, the Lowry disappeared. I can't remember the date that it went, nor the reason. I do remember that as a lazy DIY decorator, I had dripped emulsion paint onto it more than once, and it had served its purpose. I can't remember any family member or friend ever saying that they liked the painting – but we did.

Of course, now that Lowry is famous, everyone seems to appreciate him. I've visited the Lowry art gallery at Salford Quays a few times, and I've also seen his portraits and landscapes at other various galleries throughout Manchester – but I've never seen the Lowry we owned.

A recent visit to The Lowry saw us experience the art installation named 'Lowry 360'. It's a dedicated immersive experience that bounces from the walls and floor: bringing Lowry's characters to life as they crowd towards the Match – a football scene that Lowry painted at Bolton, near Manchester. The 360 has obviously been designed by a brilliant artist. It got me thinking. There are millions of brilliant artists, but being brilliant does not a genius make. When God sprinkles genius, He does so randomly. Lowry was an unlikely genius, but a genius none the less. A quiet, sometimes solitary, unfashionable, private man, Lowry didn't look the part. At the time, his paintings didn't look like the works of an accomplished artist. He abandoned the traditional painting methods that he had learned during his art education. His subject matter wasn't the traditional choice of artists. His pallet was simple and his paintings flat. And so it was that, although Lowry's art was locally recognised, his style was largely unappreciated until his middle age. Only in his later life was he acknowledged as being a talent of note. I can imagine the many people who said, "Lowry? Not for me." Now, of course, crowds queue to see his work. They stand for ages, stroking their chins, contemplating even the simplest of his sketches. I wonder, if Lowry was alive today, would he shake his head and say, "Who are you kidding? You didn't show that amount of interest in my paintings when I was a local Manchester artist."

I often visit auctions. Sometimes I just go for a trip out, and I mooch around viewing the various bits and pieces. There are often a couple of 'L S Lowry' signed prints up for sale. They normally sell for around a hundred quid or so. On Cunard ships, where people expect to buy something expensive, the same 'L S Lowry' signed prints sell for thousands. I'm reckoning that if Lowry had actually signed all these prints, it would have taken him years. I remember visiting a Manchester warehouse that shipped paintings and prints around the UK. The dealer got chatting and he told me that his father had gained Lowry's permission to print off a small number of signed copies; but the printer had done it many dozens of times over and made a good living at it. He sold me a signed 'L S Lowry' pencil copy of a football match. I've still got it somewhere. Value? No idea.

When I'm unsure if my appreciation of Lowry is being influenced by his now fashionable fame, I look back to the seventies and remember the time when I first bought that Lowry painting all those years ago. A time when he was not as famous and there was no other reason to buy his work, other than I liked it, and it fitted over the fireplace. And sometimes, I wonder, did we fling out an 'L S Lowry' original? Nah. I'm sure not, and anyway, sometimes it's better not to know.

1959-635 SELF PORTRAIT 1925

© The Lowry Collection, Salford

Mr Lowry

Bernie Shaw

The smoky North West was never the best,
Place to grow, to work and to thrive.
Factories and chimneys belching black smoke,
Made it hard to just stay alive.

But at least one man, with his brushes and pad,
Loved all the scenes, he knew what he had.
He sketched and he painted, smiled,
He was glad northern life was all around.

Mr Lowry, you captured us all,
Mr Lowry, the short and the tall.
The sick, the lazy, the lame and the quaint,
The lonely, the crazies – with five shades of paint.

They said he painted on Sundays,
And only that day.
The posh people laughed,
They were stupid that way.

Mr Lowry just smiled and said,
What can I say?
But I'm famous and rich,
Now where the hell are they?

He became more famous,
But still stayed the same,
Painting some landscapes,
Again and again.

Seascapes as well,
But he always remained,
True to himself,
Mr Lowry.

Lowry's Mother's Deathbed

Rosemary Swift

1963-5 Two People

© The Lowry Collection, Salford

Lowry: Try and get out of bed for a while, Mother. It will ease the congestion on your chest. I must admit it is quite foggy for an October night, even though there are heavy curtains to the windows.

Mother:	I have decided I am not staying around for yet another tussle with the Germans. This one has only been going on a month but mark my words there will not be a phony War as we thought last time. I shall stay in bed and give way. Your father left me to your mercy some seven years and more now – and you are just as useless a lump as you have ever been. And there's my sister, Mary, having three delicate daughters. A daughter would have pleased me.
Lowry:	I try to please you. I sit with you at night and do not do any artwork until you go to sleep.
Mother:	Huh, artworks? Is that what you call them! Scribbling on cardboard and the like, I call it! I was a proper artist, a music teacher, and yet your father never bought me a piano.
Lowry:	You could have bought one, even recently; he left you a few hundred pounds.
Mother:	That went towards his debts. He was as useless as you.
Lowry:	He employed domestic servants all through your married life so as not to disfigure your hands.
Mother:	Before my marriage that was also the case. We had domestic help. My father was very strict with his children. I appreciate I had to be also, being left to care for my siblings.
Lowry:	But you left your family home in North Manchester and moved to South Manchester, something my father arranged – first to Stretford and then to Rusholme.
Mother:	Yes, and very nice it was too – leafy Victoria Park. I sigh for it. Instead, we ended up here in Pendlebury, amongst smoky mills and factories.

59

Lowry: I admit I too missed our former home but one night on leaving the railway station, I was struck by how impressive Acme Mill looked, silhouetted against the late afternoon sky, with its windows gleaming yellow. I just had to paint it and its workers scurrying from work.

Mother: That does not mean you had to start painting similar scenes. And you can't paint figures – they look like ants. With your education you were brought up to do better than that.

Lowry: The scenes are based on places I pass through when out rent collecting. The local people are so friendly and interested in what I do. They were much friendlier again when I went to Bolton to depict men going to the local football match.

Mother: Friendly is as friendly does. I was brought up to be more reserved and proper and speak when spoken to. Although I must say I am treated locally with utmost respect for my religious views and musical talents. Anyway, I am weary of talking and beginning to choke – pass me some water to sip.

Lowry: I will just prop you up, Mother, as you are dribbling the water, and why are you looking at me with such an open-eyed stare? Mother...!

Lowry: She's gone....

Thoughts on Lowry as an Artist

Sylvia Edwards

1959-644 THE FUNERAL PARTY

© The Lowry Collection, Salford

With regard to Lowry, how fascinating it is to compare this successful painter with an equally successful and renowned novelist. While Dickens composed his colourful characters from people he observed in and around London, focusing his vivid imaginings like a pair of binoculars that opened up and expanded the complex lives he saw around him, did Lowry do the same with his art? Further, did Lowry also aim for 'difference' as his human theme, as Dickens clearly did?

   I am inclined to think not, for a number of reasons. Firstly, his painting, *Coming from the Mill*, (interpreted on the front cover of this anthology) focuses, not on people as individuals, but on the background against which they are moving. At first glance, what do we see? Do we note the figures in the foreground? Or do we note the grim greyness of the buildings behind, from which the workers look like they are hurriedly escaping? Mills and smoke dominate this painting as the backdrop. In a strange sort of way, did Lowry perhaps intend the blacks and greys of the mill setting to create the details of his characters' lives as a moving mass of humanity – instead of painting 'differences'?

Did Lowry also see his characters more as 'masses' than individuals? Did he, from talking to people on the street and collecting rents, come to regard these working people from a distance in order for him to build a composite impression of the time and what it was like to work in a factory?

Lowry's *Blitzed Site*, painted in 1942, also focused more on the wartime setting. Just a few people, without facial or bodily detail, portrayed in his usual black. Similarly, in *The Football Match* hordes of people are gathered around a local football pitch, against a sombre background of mill chimneys and dark smoke rising towards a grey sky. Odd splashes of red on buildings break up the greyness.

From *The Funeral Party*, painted in 1953, why was the man on the right facing sideways instead of frontwards, as if separated from the other characters in the picture? Had he perhaps been rejected because of what he was wearing to a funeral? A red tie? Might this image of an outcast also reflect on the turbulent relationship that Lowry had had with his late mother – an interesting thought on how Lowry's life and relationships crept into his paintings in subtle and subdued ways?

From Lowry's paintings of people do we therefore gain an impression of him as an artist who, unlike painters such as Rembrandt, regarded them from a distance, rather than close up? Was Lowry more concerned with how these throngs of people in his artwork connected with their settings? And was this why his figures were mainly shapeless, colourless – and also expressionless? Could this have been the reason why his mother also, had failed to understand where her son was coming from?

So why, as viewers of Lowry's 'matchstick' people and animals, do we feel as much emotion as we do from a 'people' close up? Why might Lowry's paintings evoke the same feelings and passions as that of other artists? It has to be the settings. As we gaze at the places in which these characters lived and worked, we surely sense the sadness of their daily lives. Their ups and downs. Troubles and traumas. The poverty that surrounded most of the people with whom Lowry came into contact. Is this where his genius lay? Would paintings of posh houses and middle-class streets have evoked as much emotion and empathy? I think not.

At a recent exhibition of Lowry's works (Lowry 360: June 2025), I found myself staring in fascination at his figures. His painted people do not smile. The *Father and Two Sons* stare out of the canvas, causing us to wonder at the challenges that may have faced them. Is there a sense of hopelessness as I look into their eyes?

The artist's own life appears to have been consumed with his characters' daily battles. He made constant reference to their perceived loneliness – describing crowds of people as "strangers to each other". As I stared into his paintings, hoping to shine a light into Lowry's heart and mind, I imagined those dark industrial landscapes as his inspiration. What drove him to paint them? And was this hard, bleak background of greater interest to him than the individuals in his pictures? It would appear so. Yet he also cared deeply about those people whose daily lives existed amongst that urban backdrop. How could he not have done, having devoted many years of his life to how he imagined theirs to be? He was surely an acute observer of the human condition.

In another section of the exhibition, this artist's seascapes and landscapes also portrayed a deep sense of loneliness. What was Lowry thinking as he painted his picture of the calm water against an almost nonexistent background? Sea, horizon and sky – the loneliness of nature?

We might also ask, did Lowry seek to portray the stark contrast between his noisy industrial scenes and the silent, mindful beauty of nature? He surely must have sensed this difference. The darkness of the mills – against the blue sky reflected from the sea? The smell – of waste, vermin and unwashed bodies – contrasted with the freshness carried along by a coastal breeze? The constant bellowing of machinery – against the gentle lapping of waves? And the touch – of dirt and grease, contrasted with the softness of sand and sea? Differences we can all empathise with.

So, my final question: how important was Lowry's art as an antidote to his own loneliness? Did he suffer from low mood, and were his paintings part of his search for emotional well-being?

We can only speculate on the private thoughts of this unique and talented artist. But one thing we can be sure of: his lasting legacy, dedicated to the strength and bravery of people who stood up to the social challenges of their time – and won!

On a Pebble Beach

Chris Barwood

1954-152 SEASCAPE

Laurence Stephen Lowry was born on the 1st November 1887, at No. 8 Barrett Street, Stretford, to Elizabeth and Robert. It was a difficult birth for his mother, who had wished for a girl and always regarded her son as a 'clumsy boy' and blamed him for her deteriorating health. She was a talented, well-respected lady with aspirations of becoming a concert pianist. Her ill health made her an irritating and nervous woman, brought up by her parents to expect high standards, particularly from her stern and controlling father who showed little if any affection towards his family.

L S Lowry's early years were spent in the leafy Manchester suburb of Victoria Park, Rusholme. The family moved to Pendlebury in 1909, when he was twenty-two years of age. Here he encountered, not the leafy streets he was used to, but a landscape of textile mills and factory chimneys looming over his new home like the Sword of Damocles: a landscape he initially hated but later became the framework of his best artistic works. He would begin to draw these dark and drab landscapes, with shadowless people who were also soulless – those today we call his 'matchstick men'.

Lowry often stated, when asked about his childhood, that he had had an unhappy one, showing no academic aptitude for schoolwork, although his father, a quiet and unobtrusive man, showed him some affection within the repressive atmosphere of the family structure, dominated by Elizabeth.

His painting was often considered naive and childlike by his contemporaries, and his mother gave him no credit at all for having "any sort of talent" and dismissed him, dying before his work was recognised as the talent we know today. After her death Lowry became depressed and neglected the upkeep of his home to such a degree that the landlord repossessed it in 1948, and he was forced to move. However, although he had very little money, he bought a house in Mottram in Longden Dale, Cheshire called 'The Elms' where he was to live the rest of his life.

With his background as dark and unhappy as it appears to have been, there is no real wonder that he was a solitary gentleman, keeping his own company for much of the time. His solace seems to have been interrupted by his love of the loneliness and tranquillity he found within his treks to Berwick-upon-Tweed and Sunderland where he spent many holidays painting wonderful scenes of beaches, ports and coal mines. Vast expanses of sea and sand were portrayed in some of his well-known pictures.

It is against this backdrop that I have set this fictional story called 'On A Pebble Beach'. He was staying at the Seaburn Hotel in Sunderland and would go down to the beach each day to paint. He was a secretive and mischievous man who enjoyed telling stories and anecdotes full of humour and he often set out to deceive. Although he insisted that he had "never had a woman", he left his audience wondering what was true and what was imaginary – and on this note our story begins….

On a Pebble Beach

The young man, pencil in hand, pad on knee, watched intensely as the shallow waves tapped in and out over the stony, sandless beach. His eyes glistened with the tears which crept silently from his red eyes. He looked a sad spectacle, just sitting.

His heart ached; he wished he had spoken more easily to the young woman who had stolen his heart, but he could not bring himself to admit to her the feelings which had stirred within his breast at that meeting, or the sickening churning of his stomach which began at the very thought of her.

A picture of beauty, such as he had never seen before, emblazoned on his brain – her gentle face a vision which had captured his young heart. She had walked up to him that sunny, hot day, with no clouds in the sky, and had stood, watching him for some time before he realised she was there.

"Your pictures are very beautiful," she had said, in a quiet tuneful voice. "I wondered if I could purchase one from your collection. I do so love them," she had continued.

Stuttering and stammering, Lowry had answered, "Yes, yes, of course, by all means, although I – I don't really have a collection, just one or two sketches, please take one, no charge."

"How much are they?" she had insisted "I have enough money to pay; I am in service at the big house and am able to pay my way. I would not wish you to give me one for nothing. By the way, I'm Leanora Simpson." She had held out a white hand, with long fingers and short, well-manicured nails.

He had transfixed upon this vision standing before him for several seconds before offering his hand to her. "I'm Laurence," he continued.

"It's very nice to meet you, Laurence," was her reply.

"If we could meet tomorrow, here, I will bring you one of my best paintings, one which I really like," he had continued.

"Yes, that would be lovely, but I really do insist on paying for it," Leanora had stated firmly." And I won't take no for an answer." She had laughed.

"Yes, yes, fine." He had fumbled for his words again – and at this point, they had parted company.

The Following Day

His mind was so jumbled as he had made his way home the previous evening. He was feeling as light as a feather and had skipped along the pavement back to his hotel with a newfound spirit in his soul.

He waited patiently all that morning, hoping Leanora would come, but alas to no avail. She did not arrive and finally he decided to put his pen and pad away for the afternoon and go and find somewhere to have a cup of tea and something to eat. He had not eaten at all that morning: his stomach was churning as if he were on a merry-go-round, and a feeling of nausea had taken over his body.

As the bell on the shop door tinkled, he walked into the café, each table spread with clean red and white gingham tablecloths. The café was nearly empty, with only two old ladies sitting chatting in one corner, drinking a ubiquitous cup of tea from small china cups.

He ordered a cheese sandwich and a glass of water and sat down by the window so he could see if Leanora passed. He was afraid he had missed her or made a mistake about the arrangements. Just as the waitress brought his order, Leanora passed the window, hurrying along the pavement, her hand on her head, holding onto her hat as the wind blew her along.

Jumping up from his seat, he rushed the short distance to the door, opened it in haste and shouted to her, hoping his voice would be carried on the wind to her delicate ears.

She turned around, a beam on her face as she recognised the caller. She made her way towards him, crying. "Oh Laurence, I am so sorry, I just could not get away." A note of desperation in her voice.

"Come and join me for tea," he replied.

"Oh, I would love to," she exclaimed.

He ordered a pot of tea and a second cheese sandwich, and the couple sat and chatted about paintings, their jobs, their love of the sea, but never a word was said about feelings or even meeting again. Eventually, Leanora got up, thanked Laurence for his kind gift of a small painting featuring a boat laid half in and half out of the water and, with a gentle hand upon his shoulder, wished him well for the future – then left his life, never to return.

Laurence watched as Leanora strolled away from the tea shop, away from the sea and sand, and away from him. He felt he should have asked to see her again, or maybe for a contact address so he could write to her in the future, but he hadn't, and so his one and only true love was lost in the sands of time and they were destined never to meet again. Although, year after year, he visited the same spot in the hope their paths would cross again, this was not to be, and as we now know, L S Lowry, artist of great renown, never did marry. But he would always have a gleam in his eye whenever asked why he had not married.

Philistines Aren't Born

Sketch by Colin Balmer

SCENE: *Teatime in a modern semi-detached council house..*

BILLY: Dad, what's all the noise about some artist from Pendlebury? Mrs Arfield, our arts and crafts teacher, goes on and on about Alice Lowry. She showed us some pictures. They weren't like proper art with portraits and landscapes. More like I used to do when I was in Year 3. Was Alice just a clever kid? I did a search, but I can't find her with Google or Wikipedia or anything.

DAD: Don't let them teachers give you the impression they know everything, Billy. I never thought a lot of them when I was at school – especially the arty types who liked to feel superior.

BILLY: But, Dad, if she were that good, why ain't she on search engines?

DAD: You won't find Alice Lowry on the web because it's Laurence Stephen Lowry, see – L S – not Alice. He was a Salford rent man. A lot of people say they like his drawings and a lot of people have paid a fortune for some of 'em. It comes down to what I call The Emperor's New Clothes syndrome or Sycophants and Underpants. It happens a lot with snobs who like to appear to be art experts.

BILLY: So what do you know about him, Dad?

DAD: Before you were born, some blokes wrote a song about him drawing matchstick men and kids. It was 'Top of the Pops' in its day. A simple catchy tune, easy words – that you could even hear,

70

and kids sung along with them. It was the classic example of food for the masses. Some critics have argued it was promoted as a reaction to the reactionary Sex Pistols and The Clash. Same Emperor's New Clothes issue – philosophers at it again, making a theory out of what is just for fun.

BILLY: So he was sung about as a folk hero? That's daft, isn't it?

DAD: No. It's life. Someone saw money in his paintings; someone jumped on the bandwagon and made money with a simple song. People liked the ear candy. Their choice. Like his pictures.

BILLY: Arty Arfield had us analysing some pictures for debate. Some of the posh kids said they were brilliant. Half the class said they were dead simple, like anyone could do an 'Alice' – sorry I keep forgettin'. They say L S Lowry was taking the p... mickey out of the art world. Was he the best or a joker?

DAD: Well, Son, that shows there's a fine line between paradigm and parody, doesn't it?

BILLY: I suppose so, Dad. You've got your opinions and use arty words to explain yourself – kids in class laugh at me when I say words like 'parody' and 'paradigm' but Arty Arfield gives me house points and I'm embarrassed in front of my mates, so I don't say much.

DAD: Don't be afraid to be different and say what you feel. A great man called Karl Marx said "question everything". Just 'cause teacher says something, don't swallow it blindfold, (*chuckle*) and that's a mixed metaphor.

BILLY: Great, Dad. What should I say about Lowry? She said he painted all his pictures with only five colours.

DAD: Say he must have been a skinflint. Proper grand masters would invest in a decent palette. Or ask what's so clever about that? Your TV shows all colours using only RGB – which is red, green and blue pixels. Or, when I was buying printed brochures, my print company used only CYM combination of inks. That's cyan, yellow and magenta.

BILLY: I think my mates'll have a laugh at that. The pictures look like cartoons anyway. Perhaps he would have been good at comics. Thanks, Dad.

DAD: No problem, Billy. But remember, just because he comes from Salford, he's not necessarily the world's best. It's fine to be proud of your roots but be careful they've not grown from seeds of sectarianism, racialism, prejudice, parochial chauvinism or bigoted, arrogant jingoism. Irrespective of our talents, we all deserve equal and fair treatment.

Coming from the Mill

Reflection by Sylvia Edwards

1958-4 Coming from the Mill

© The Lowry Collection, Salford

These short fictional snapshots focus on Lowry's fascinating painting, *Coming from the Mill*. Lowry created this painting in 1930 and, though described by the artist as his "most characteristic mill scene", it was not truly representative of any specific location. This oil-on-canvas artwork was apparently inspired by real life observation of Pendlebury station.

It is said that every person has a story to tell. What stories, or indeed secrets, may be hidden behind some of Lowry's mill workers? What situations might they be going home to? Intriguing questions. So, from this scene I ask what might some of Lowry's unique 'matchstick' characters be either thinking or saying as they escape from the heat and noise of the place where they have spent a long and exhausting day?

We can only imagine their troubled thoughts…

Gladys joined the throng streaming out into the fresh air: breathing it in as deeply as her lungs would allow. Never before had she felt so tired…and dirty. Both her legs and back ached from many hours of standing. From 6.30 this morning. And she had hardly eaten. She hurried along, afraid to think what she might find when she picked up her young son, Tommy, from her next-door neighbour. His dreadful, racking cough! Gladys uttered a silent prayer as she rushed along, her own footsteps echoing like distant drums alongside hundreds of others on the cobbled street. *"Please, God, don't let it be anything serious?"* After all, she couldn't afford a doctor. They were only for the posh folk.

Percy hobbled along as best he could on his bad leg. His dear mother! How would she be today when he got back? He had left her in bed after having fed her some porridge oats before he left that morning. Ten hours ago! And she couldn't even get up to make herself a pot of tea. All he could do was leave her a glass of water, with a slice of bread and jam on the bedside table. He hoped she had managed to use the potty under the bed. Yesterday when he had got home, he had found the sheets wet and dirty from her 'accidents'. The smell, as he had opened the front door, had sickened him. He sighed as he made his way along the cobbled street, almost dreading what he might find. What was he to do? How much longer could he leave her alone to go to work? Yet, how could he not? How could they live without his meagre wages from the factory?

Agnes was trembling as she followed the throng up the alleyway and out onto the cobbled street. She breathed deeply and held onto her torn dress with one hand, trying to understand how it had happened. In just a few seconds, perhaps while she had not been concentrating enough, the spinning machine had swung forwards – trapping her skirt. She had screamed out, and the foreman had rushed over to

74

cut the trapped material from its jaw-like grip. Agnes shivered as she walked, thinking how much worse the accident could have been. What if it had been her hand? Or her foot? Trapped in that monster. Another accident like that and she might never work again. Then where would she be? Tears rolled down her cheeks as Agnes hurried home to the children, hoping desperately that they were safe, and feeling guilty about leaving them to see to themselves after school. But what else could she do? She had to work! With Jimmy having been killed in the war, she had no choice! No choice at all!

Ernie hurried along the street of fellow workers, yet, of strangers also – trying to control his morbid thoughts. He imagined the scene as he opened his front door. His wife would have made a pot of stew again. It was all they managed to eat these days. He was sick of it. His children would be shouting and arguing. No bloody peace! He had spent all day thinking what best to do about the problem. They already had five. How could they possibly afford another babby? The wailing! Sleepless nights! Another mouth to feed! No! No! So, he had made up his mind. The old woman who lived down the back alley. Yes – for a shilling or two, she would surely take care of the problem; and cheaper in the long run than having yet another bloody child. But would his wife agree? Ernie pursed his lips and clenched his fists as he turned into his dingy street. She had to agree. He would force her. He was the boss after all…and there was no other way out.

Betty held back tears as she hurried along, following in the footsteps of her fellow workers. Somehow the hymn they had sung yesterday, in church, had come into her mind again. She sang it now, gazing upwards into the grey sky, wondering if God was watching over her. Did he know? *"…and was Jerusalem builded here, amongst those dark, satanic mills?"* she sang to herself. Satanic mills! Until last week she had not realised that Satan existed. That he could indeed be as human as she was! But he did exist. And he

75

was here. Only this morning, the foreman had called her into his private office and threatened to sack her – told her that she was too slow in her work. As if that was not enough, to her shame – and horror, he had stood over her and felt at her breasts through the thin fabric of her blouse. All the time leering at her as he did so. She had not dared to resist him. There was no-one she could tell. No-one! Except God, of course. Did God know about the human Satans in this world? Tears rolled down her cheeks as she walked along the cobbled street – past the satanic mills, head down, hoping that no-one would notice her, while dreading what the morrow would bring.

Harold coughed and spat into the dirty scrap of rag that served as a handkerchief. What was he to do? He had ignored the obvious signs for a while. But for how long could he go on turning a blind eye? He folded the lump of rag and thrust it into his pocket, having first noted with alarm the green phlegm smeared across it. Was there blood mixed in? He could not be sure. He did not dare to look.

It had been raining and the cobbles were still damp from the recent shower, he noticed, following in the footsteps of his fellow workers – through the factory gate and out onto the dingy street. What did the doctors call it? Brown lung! Yes, that was it. And no bloody wonder! Why would anybody in their right mind want to spend all day in that dreadful airless place? Yet, what choice did he have, with a wife and six kiddies to feed and clothe?

How ironic too! Four sodding years of war, and he had come through it with hardly a scratch, having watched his comrades fall and die in front of him. But for what purpose had God bothered to save him from a bullet or a shell, if only for him to die now from a horrible disease? At least, if he had perished in the war, his wife might have had some kind of pension. But now, as it was…?

He gazed up at the grey sky, ominous with clouds that looked about to explode again. Was that a face…floating amongst the clouds? Was He there? Somewhere. Could

God read his thoughts, and was He already waiting? Would it soon be time to meet his maker?

Fanny stared at the cobbles as she walked. Her friend, Elsie, walked beside her, chattering on about bread. But Fanny was not really listening. All she could do was utter the occasional "yes", and nod, as tears threatened. How much longer could she stand it? Her friend had no idea of her life outside of the mill. All day they had stood together, operating the machine in the spinning room. For twelve solid hours. Sometimes she just wanted to throw herself onto that monstrous lump of moving metal – and let it squash the life out of her.

But she couldn't. Walter would be waiting now…waiting for her to get home. He would go down to the pub as he always did. Drink himself delirious…before coming home and thumping the life out of her, as he did every night – making sure that no-one could see the bruises. And for no other reason than she was there. Simply there. His personal punchbag. Something to take his anger and frustration out on.

But it wasn't her fault that he had lost an arm in the war and couldn't find a proper job. It wasn't her fault that he spent all day at home, watching the kids, while she tried her best to keep them all fed and decently clothed. Nor was it her fault that they wouldn't be able to pay Mr Lowry, the rent man, when he came by early this evening. Yet…it would end up being her fault, of course, as he took the rent money to spend on his booze.

As Fanny reached the dilapidated hovel that was her home, she stopped as she saw Mr Lowry talking to her husband. What lame excuse had he given the rent man today? And for how much longer would that dear, kind man continue to wait patiently for his money? How much longer – before they got thrown out onto the street?

Elsie concentrated on placing one foot in front of the other as she walked beside Fanny. Whatever would her friend think if she knew? The shame! How tempted she was to just turn the other way and never go home again. Was homelessness a better option than what she had? But how could she? What would happen to little Doris if she left? Besides, Alf would surely find her. And then what would happen? The thought of his fury bearing down upon her caused her to almost faint with fear.

"Bye, Fanny…see you tomorrow." A few minutes later, Elsie had reached her house. Number 13. She closed her eyes and leaned against the door frame, wanting to sink down onto the stone step. Alf would be inside, waiting to take over. All smiles…and outward pretence. He would have supper ready on the table. He would have Doris fed, bathed and ready for bed. He would have…

She opened the front door. Stepped inside. Hugged her child. After supper, as day faded and night took over, Alf nodded across the table…indicating for her to go upstairs and get ready, as usual. She needed to look the part that she was about to play. Her dress lay on the bed – placed there by Alf. Her make-up sat on the dressing table.

A few minutes later, Elsie stared at her different self in the mirror. The self that she would never be able to recognise – or accept as long as she lived. The scarlet dress – that revealed the shape of her breasts through the thin satin. The high-heeled shoes. Bright red lipstick. Rouged cheeks. Her other self – the self that could never, ever belong to her. The self of the night worker! A world away from the daytime self that Fanny and other fellow workers saw every day at the mill.

The tart! She covered herself with the black cloak, wondering as she did so, how much longer she could hide from the world. She peeped into little Doris's bedroom, listening for a moment to her child's steady breathing. Then she made her way downstairs, took a deep breath …and met the cruel determination in Alf's eyes.

At last, Elsie opened the front door, closed it behind her...and let herself slowly merge into the dark and dangerous blackness of the Salford streets.

Tea With Mother

Sketch by Paul Muldoon

The familiar sound of the Yale lock closing in its catch was heard as Mr Lowry returned from work.

Mother: (*The voice of his bed-ridden mother from upstairs.*) Laurence! Laurence! Is that you, our Laurence?

Laurence: (*Shouted upstairs*) Yes, it's me, Mother, back home from work. (*Under his breath*) Fetch me a cup of tea.

Mother: (*Shouted from upstairs*) Fetch me a cup of tea, will you?

Laurence: (*In a quiet voice*) Please! Just one sugar.

Mother: Just one sugar!

Laurence: (*Shouting*) I know, I know! I've been making tea long enough for you to know that!

Laurence takes the tea upstairs.

A few minutes later. Mother sips.

Mother: Ahh! Thank you, Son. (*Slight pause*) Had a good day at work, have you? Robbing people of their hard-earned brass?

Laurence: It's called 'rent', Mother. Everybody has to pay it, even us. That's why I go to work, to earn money to pay our rent, and buy tea, sugar and everything else in this house.

Mother: Your father works! Don't be such a martyr.

Laurence: Yes, I know he does, but we can't run this house on his pittance.

Mother: Well, get yourself another job instead of wasting your time, scribbling those silly pictures. We'd be better off!

Laurence: We get by, Mother; and they're not silly pictures. They're *art*, my art and my hobby.

Mother: That's not art! Smoking chimneys and factories, bent-over matchstick men; they're rubbish! Have you ever seen a Renoir? Now, that's art!

Laurence: Yes, I've seen a Renoir, and it's good, but it's a Renoir, not a Lowry! Look out of the window, Mother, do you see the Eiffel Tower? The Coliseum or Saint Mark's Square? No! It's not Paris, Rome or Venice out there! It's Salford, our Salford, so that's *my* subject, *my* muse.

Mother: Father showed me your latest picture – just as bad as all the rest. *Going to the Match* you called it. It's a pity you don't join in the match like other young men instead of 'painting' as you call it, more like scribbling I call it. At least make an effort to paint like the Grand Masters.

Laurence: They belong to their own schools, Mother: Impressionists, pre-Raphaelites, and the rubbish they call Cubism. I belong to my own school, self-taught, and I live here in Salford, so I'm a one-man school. I call it Salfordism, or better still, Lowryism. Now, drink your tea and I'll go and make dinner.

Mother: What are we having?

Laurence: Egg and chips.

Mother: Oh, good.

Laurence: (*Under his breath*) – Don't forget the salt and vinegar…

Mother: (*Barked as he leaves the room*) – Don't forget the salt and vinegar…!

Favourite Piece of Art by Lowry

Rosemary Swift

1959-642 THE FIGHT

© The Lowry Collection, Salford

Although L S Lowry's portraits are interesting (red-rimmed eyes, etc), I am more attracted to the crowd scenes in many of his paintings, my favourite being *A Procession*, painted in 1938, where the backs of a crowd of people are depicted watching a banner-led procession on an elevated street in Pendleton, a suburb of Salford. It is so atmospheric, you feel you want to run towards it and catch the music no doubt being played.

For the first decade of my life, I lived in inner-city Manchester where many a religious procession took place. It could be the regular Sunday morning Boys' Brigade parading through the streets playing bugles or the annual Walks into central Manchester on both Whit Monday and Whit Friday and parochial walks on a Trinity Sunday afternoon where local Churches were either led by a Brass Band or a Pipe Band. My Parish of St. Anne's was so large we had both a home-based brass band and home-based pipe band to accompany us. Also, it was an annual treat to go and watch the Italian community walk in Ancoats carrying shoulder high large religious statues surrounded by hundreds of fresh lilies. Whereas a tuppenny cornet was the order of the day when Granelli's brought a van to the streets around my home in Beswick on summer evenings, when we were in the heart of the Italian ice cream parlours around Ancoats on this annual occasion we were treated to a twist with raspberry sauce.

My Dad, many years ago, bought a copy of L S Lowry's *A Fight* – painted circa 1935 – for my brother Steve's home in Hayfield which features four men and a woman, where one of the men is ramming a hat onto another man's head with the other two men stood watching and the woman turning away. For my father this depicted my four brothers and me.

However, I have to stress, much as I appreciate the works of L S Lowry, I prefer the Flemish crowd scenes of the works of the Brueghel family being Pieter the Elder (circa 1525–1569); Pieter the Younger (1564–1638); Jan the Elder (1568–1625) and Jan the Younger (1601–1678); one of which, *A Village Fair* (based on a Village Festival in honour of

83

St. Hubert and St. Anthony) by Pieter Brueghel the Younger, is displayed in my home. Visitors could look at it for hours and still find a feature of an action taking place. Another favourite of mine for busy scenes are the works of Hieronymus Bosch (circa 1450–1516).

But of course Lowry's crowd scenes are more evocative because he is contemporary, inasmuch that I recognise in my lifetime the scenes of crowds shopping on Pendlebury Market or leaving football grounds, or when the hooter goes at the end of a working day and folk pour out of the factories and mills, or indeed, as I mention above, rushing to watch a procession bringing folk out of their homes - free entertainment being thin on the ground in those pre-TV days.

Lowry Grew on Me

Jackie Blades

When I was little, I lived in a village called Bellingham, in the wilds of Northumberland. Our house was the last in the village, on the road up to Otterburn. The view from my bedroom window was completely rural: fields, sheep and a rustic, stone-built farm.

My dad got a job in Salford when I was six. I will never forget my first view of the conurbation of Manchester as we drove down the M62, as it sprawled out in front of us. It was night time and there were lights EVERYWHERE! "For every streetlight you can see…" my mum told me, "there are about ten houses, probably about thirty or so people." I was absolutely flabbergasted: all those lights, all those houses, all those people!

My mum took a job working for the council, undertaking a survey about the housing and provisions for disabled people within the city. It was a baptism of fire for her, having been brought up in a middle-class family in Kent, visiting poor working-class families living on the breadline in terrible conditions. This was prior to the slum clearance in the 1960's. She was extremely upset when she saw the poverty that many of Salford's most vulnerable and needy citizens had to endure.

One theme that ran through almost every single household was the pride that these Salfordians felt for their famous artist – L S Lowry. Pride of place above cluttered mantelpieces were reproductions of Lowry's paintings.

Personally, at the time, I wasn't much impressed by his unique style and subject matter. Our household had oil paintings on the walls painted by my grandfather, of land and seascapes, totally different to Lowry's style.

In 1978, the song 'Matchstalk Men and Matchstalk Cats and Dogs' rocketed into the charts, and I began to feel a grudging respect for him and for what his art stood for. Even though I was born in the North East, for most of my life I have lived in Salford. And now I too hold L S Lowry and the Salford he captured all those years ago in high regard.

The history of our city has been bulldozed over during the past century and much of the original industrial lifestyle of thousands of Salford's people has gone, but Lowry captured parts of our heritage in his simple brush strokes which would have been lost otherwise.

He was an artist of his time and captured Salfordians and Mancunians during the early 20th Century – before guns and wars and untold slaughter maimed our population.

Les Riley: A Life in Swinton

Sketch by Warren Davies

On Monday, February 23rd, 1976, in the Woods Hospital at Glossop, one of Britain's most celebrated and original artists, Laurence Stephen Lowry, died. He was aged 88.

Scene: 10-year-old Harry bursts into his parents' house, throws his satchel onto the floor then slumps into his favourite chair to be greeted by his dad.

DAD: Hello Son! How's school?

HARRY: Boring! All afternoon the teacher has been tellin' us about some artist, Les Riley, who died this morning. Is it true that he lived in Swinton?

DAD: Yeah! That's right Son! In fact, he lived at 117 Station Road...not far from us, just up the road from your Auntie Betty.

HARRY: What, near Aldi and Morrisons where you and me mam go shopping?

DAD: Yeah! Where me and your mam go shopping.

HARRY: Was he born in Swinton?

DAD: No.

HARRY: Why not?

DAD: Because...er...er he was born at Barrett Street, Old Trafford.

HARRY: Well why did he move to Swinton then?

DAD: Well Son. The story goes that owing to financial hardship, he and his parents could no longer afford to live at 14, Pine Grove, Victoria Park, Manchester.

Narrator: On May 4th,1909, the Lowrys moved to Station Road.

HARRY: Is that Victoria Park, just down the road...the one we play football in?

DAD: No, Son! The Victoria Park I'm talking about was a private estate in Manchester; it had big gates to keep out people like us.

HARRY: Did he like it here?

DAD: His mother, Elizabeth, didn't. In fact, she hated the area and the people. He, at first hated it too.

Narrator: One day in 1916, Lowry missed a train from Pendlebury to Manchester. As he left the station, (in a sour mood), he noticed the Acme Spinning Company's Mill. Hundreds of hunched black figures were pouring out in a steady stream: this was Lowry's epiphany. For over thirty years, he dedicated his painting to industrial landscapes. What if Lowry had not moved to Swinton? Would he have been as famous?

HARRY: Did he do anything else but paint?

DAD: Yeah, he was a rent collector for over forty years; tenants had to pay him rent so they could live there.

HARRY: Ten-ants? How could ants pay him?

DAD: Oh, never mind!

HARRY: I thought you said Les was a painter?

DAD: He was! But it was a long time before he became famous and made any money.

Narrator: For nearly thirty years – from 1910 to 1939 – Lowry painted without recognition of his art. It would be until the '40s before he made a profit, until the '50s for recognition, and until the late '60s for high prices.

88

HARRY: So why wasn't he living in Swinton until he died this morning?

DAD: Well Son, circumstances change, and we change with them.

HARRY: Sir Stan says...?

DAD: Never mind bloody Sir Stan. Both his parents had died in that house and he felt lost. Unfortunately, he neglected the property for so long that neighbours complained about it lowering the tone of the road.

Narrator: Lowry's landlord, Louis Duffy, had been aware for some time of the deteriorating relationship between Lowry and his neighbours. His solution was to offer Lowry his much smaller house at 72 Chorley Road in exchange for 117 Station Road. The deal was agreed in June 1947. Lowry had lived there for nearly forty years.

HARRY: Did he have to move because he was scruffy?

DAD: Yeah, I think so. He moved only around the corner, somewhere on Chorley Road. He was there for just over a year. I don't think he liked it.

HARRY: Where did Les move to?

Narrator: In August,1948, Lowry agreed to buy 'The Elms' in Mottram-in-Longdendale, where he would spend the rest of his life.

DAD: Mutch...er...Motch...er...somewhere far away from Swinton.

HARRY: Will you be going to Les's funeral?

DAD: No. By the way, Son, his name is *Laurence Stephen Lowry*, or *L S Lowry* for short...not... Les Riley!

HARRY: I shall tell the teacher tomorrow!

Narrator: L S Lowry was a one-off; a true individual who ploughed his own furrow through life. He never compromised his art or his individuality. For years, this eccentric and enigmatic character trudged the streets of Salford, without prescience of any fame or fortune which would arrive later...much later. His paintings would be later exhibited in America, Australia, Canada and New Zealand. Not bad for a rent collector who lived in Swinton.

Harold Riley's Friendship with L S Lowry

Rosemary Swift

1959-643 HOUSE ON THE MOOR

© The Lowry Collection, Salford

Salford-born artist Harold Riley, after meeting when a student, was to become a great friend of L S Lowry and visited him on many occasions at The Elms (Lowry's Mottram-in-Longdendale home from 1948), spending hours within Lowry's home studio.

On other occasions, they would take the bus to lunch at Sam's Chop House in Central Manchester or for a change (although Lowry was a man of habit) to the Alma Lodge in the area of Heaviley, Stockport.

This continued until Lowry's death (due to pneumonia) in 1976 at the Woods Hospital, Glossop. Lowry is buried next to his parents at Southern Cemetery in Chorlton-cum-Hardy, Manchester.

For many years, both Lowry and Riley were interested in capturing the street scenes around their hometown. At one of Riley's exhibitions, he displayed a series of art stored within Lowry's home studio in Mottram. At another exhibition, Riley showed photos of L S Lowry including the two of them playing football. Harold commented that Lowry was quite a good dribbler as he was very knock-kneed, and you didn't know which way he was going!

Incidentally, L S Lowry holds the record for rejecting the most British honours – five! An OBE in 1955 and a CBE in 1961, a Knighthood in 1968 and the Order of the Companions of Honour (CH) in 1972 and 1976. Riley said Lowry had told him it was not that he had anything against the system; it was that he did not wish to have anything

Riley summed it up that Lowry had been a very private person and confided in very few people. It would seem he was also like this in his relationships with people he did communicate with, saying something to one and something different to another. He denied having any living relatives and yet he had a lady cousin who had been very close to him in their youth being of similar age and they were still in touch up to his death. Yet he did not leave her anything in his Will, leaving his fortune to a young lady he had befriended through her mother who had written many years previously saying they had the same surname as Lowry. Of a mercurial nature, some would even say Lowry was sly and mischievous.

FOOTNOTE *Harold Riley died 18 April 2023 (sixteen days after the death of Archie Swift, MBE – husband of Rosemary). They too were good friends through rugby and Archie doing plumbing and heating works at Riley's home at Irlams o'th' Height. The local Catholic church where both had funeral services a week apart displays many items of Riley's work, such as stations of the cross and a painting entitled 'Madonna of Manchester'.*

Reflections on Mother

Mary Young

Perhaps what L S Lowry may have said in reflection on his life and relationship with his mother…

A missed train was the beginning of a dream I had to bring the industrial scene of Pendlebury to life on the map of Britain as no one had previously done so.

I did not want to be like every other artist before me, but studied and took inspiration from them nevertheless.

I used the twilight hours to hone my craft as it was the only time when I could be free from my dear mother's constant ridicule of my simple offerings as an artist.

If only she had had more faith in my uniqueness. She would have had the opportunity to boast about the famous son I became. But no, she did not, could not appreciate or understand what I was trying to convey, either subliminally or deliberately in the simplicity of the paintings of my 'matchstalk' men, women and children. She had wanted a Rembrandt, a Van Gogh to boast of to her friends, to society in general.

Perhaps if my mother had succeeded in her quest for notoriety as a concert pianist she may have thought or behaved differently. After all, wasn't she inadvertently being told that she wasn't good enough, just as she was persistently telling me that I wasn't good enough to become a noted artist? In effect it was almost as if, subconsciously, she wanted me to fail as she felt she had failed in her quest to achieve notoriety as a concert pianist. Perhaps she could not bear to think that the son who she considered to be uneducated, unremarkable, could ever achieve the notoriety that she herself had failed to achieve.

I loved my mother for who she was, but it seemed to me that her love for me was conditional in that I had to earn it, had to prove myself worthy of it. How sad that I now have that proof, now that she is no longer here. I can just picture the soirées she would have held to boast of "Our dear Laurence's success". I would more than likely have caught the scene on canvas.

Perhaps the way my mother mothered me subconsciously contributed to my never marrying or having a family of my own.

My matchstick men, women and children are or were perhaps a reflection of how, regardless of lack of material wealth, one could be relatively happy, just getting on with day to day, mundane existence, accepting their lot in life. Some, perhaps, harboured dreams of a life of affluence for themselves and/or their children as I'm sure my mother did for her only son. Their reasons for wanting this I'm sure differed vastly from my mother's in that they mostly just dreamed of having enough to live a normal life, having enough to feed and clothe their children. My mother, on the other hand, wanted her son to be known in society for something about which she could boast to her affluent, influential friends.

My love for my mother was unconditional, simply because she was my mother. It saddens me to think that she could not love and appreciate me for my own qualities, despite my little idiosyncrasies, as I loved her despite knowing that I could never measure up to what she wanted for her only child, for him to become 'something in society'.

If only she had lived to see my success in my chosen field, I may have finally given her a reason to love me and to appreciate me for who I really am.

For myself, I hope and pray that I remained true to myself right to the very end.

Lowry: The Bridge Painter

Colin Balmer

Laurence Hardcastle could not see much of a future in Pendleton in the late fifties. At nineteen, he had already suffered four years of misery and dirt in Agecroft pit, with little prospect of promotion to deputy. He had discussed working on the docks with a few of the lads in the White Lion but could not see much of an improvement. Long hours, hard work and bitter, war-wrecked old men commanded a regime lacking interest or imagination. Old before their time, it seemed the older generation begrudged teenagers like Larry the excitement of the dancehalls and rock and roll. Society called these war survivors 'heroes' but they had seen the reality of the conflict and few claimed anything heroic from their experience. They envied the 'brave new world' the baby boomers enjoyed – and showed their resentment to these "bloody lazy Teddy boys".

Fathers and sons did not talk, even when the younger followed his parent into work. Sure, Larry had his pleasures away from the pit, at the match, at the Palais, and crib or 9-card Don in the vault of the Lion, but there was always something missing. So it was that in 1958 he told the deputy where to stick his shovel and walked out to fill his lungs with the smog-choked air.

Kirsty, with whom he had jived at the Palais, had regaled him with tales of the crisp fresh air in Scotland's glens and mountains, so he bought a single train ride to Glasgow with not much more than hope and a cardboard suitcase.

The city did not offer much more than he had left behind in Salford – Clydebank docks had suffered a similar blitz in 1941. Heavy industry in shipbuilding was equally soul-destroying. This was not the escape he was looking for.

After a few temporary jobs as he travelled east, Larry wound up in the work he knew – in the Fife coalfields, not only underground but also under the river Forth. But Scotland's coal industry was in decline and offered no future.

He was lodged with Ma Moira MacTavish, whose husband, Tommy, suggested the youngster look for a job on the Forth railway bridge. He was successful and celebrated his good fortune with lungs filled with clean, fresh sea air. This purging air would blow away the fumes of the paint as he joined the gang of painters maintaining the mammoth steel structure, 365 days a year. A Salford lad with a paint brush, Larry was sarcastically branded "The Sassenach Lowry" by Jack McGregor, a rare, educated tyrant of a foreman. He would climb to the apex of each bridge tower and revel from his exalted position, calling down to the Sassenach, "Hey, Lowry, get that brush movin'. Ye're no paintin' pretty pictures the noo. Girrrderrrs! Girrrderrrs! Girrrderrrs!" Growling like a sore-headed grizzly bear.

But Larry could breathe. And breathing awoke his imagination. The views across the Firth of Forth and serene quiet at the altitude set his creativity to a flood. An idea first occurred to Larry/Lowry as he looked down from his perch 360 feet above the Firth of Forth. The magnificent panorama from here had been exciting when he joined the maintenance gang as a novice painter. Now experienced, with a degree of responsibility, he smiled, recalling the first job that apprentices were given was to "just paint the rivets until you master your craft": it was estimated that the bridge contained something like seven million. He had soon found out that the red oxide paint, known as 'Forth Bridge Red', was the same for the whole steel structure, nearly two and a half miles long, and rivets were not given individual attention.

In the 1970s he had spent long years on the one job and wanted to get away from the repetitive task of painting this bridge. No sooner finished at the North Queensferry end – they had to start again on the Edinburgh side. Painting the red bridge now accounted for all his working life and he wanted to escape his personal *'rock of Sisyphus'* to be wild and free – to see more of the world and experience unimagined pleasures.

"Once the girrrderrrs in this pier are finished," mocking his tormentor, he told himself, "I will design a better way to do this and put it to the railway so everybody can have it easier."

But he had McGregor, the structural inspector, to by-pass first. He preciously guarded all lines of communication with the bridge management and owners. In the past, whenever Larry had wanted to talk to someone higher up, McGregor had insisted he put it in writing and he himself would see it was passed on. Strangely, nothing ever came of the painter's suggestions.

Duncan, his landlady's son, was a maintenance engineer on a North Sea oil rig – making a small fortune in the process. During one of their late-night pub sessions, they had compared paintwork on the rigs with that on Larry's bridge. Surely the technology must be transferable. Larry had spent weeks writing up a plan – from stripping the 120 years of paint layers back, sand blasting bare metal and applying a glass flake epoxy paint. It would be necessary to shield the work from the environment and even hand paint where the spray guns could not reach. A massive undertaking in itself, but McGregor would surely stop the plan getting off the ground anyway. A wasted effort!

Another alcoholic indulgence put a plan in Larry's mind. On a weekend in July with pleasant weather, he went to the local IKEA in Edinburgh and invested in a Kleppstad double-door wardrobe. Before his shift started on Monday, he took the flat-pack and assembled it against the tower he was working on. He drew from the plentiful supply of red paint and blended the wardrobe into the bridge structure, then waited for McGregor's morning inspection round.

"Mr McGregor, could you come and check this latest batch of paint?" he asked.

97

"Aye, Mr Lowry, laddie," came a patronising response to the middle-aged artisan from the inspector.

"Just here, in the paint locker."

McGregor stepped into the wardrobe.

"I canna see onything," was the last he said before the door slammed shut and Larry turned the key.

He was still shouting and banging inside the red IKEA box as it floated out on the tide, down the Forth and into the North Sea.

'The Lowry Plan', as the new painting scheme became known, was accepted by the board after six months of deliberation and the ten-year project was completed in 2011, at a cost of £30 million – the original bridge had cost only £3 million to build in 1889 and taken six years. It was not expected that the bridge would need repainting for another twenty years.

Lowry (Larry) Hardcastle from Salford, former bridge painter, was last heard of bungee jumping off a bridge in New Zealand to celebrate his fiftieth birthday, spending his employee incentive bonus. Masters of ocean-going vessels and pilots entering the Firth of Forth are careful to avoid a new shipping hazard which looks like a red, rectangular buoy.

The gods condemned Sisyphus to push a rock up the hill but it kept rolling back down again.

Polite for Patricia

Sketch by Catherine Grant-Salmon
September 3rd, 1975

Albert and Brenda are having breakfast while listening to Pete Murray's Open House show on Radio Two. They hear the flap of their post box and then the heavy thud of a daily newspaper, Brenda s magazine and the Swinton and Pendlebury Journal.

It was so good to finally be able to read and relax at leisure, having both retired from jobs at the Chloride factory and the Dunfermline Building Society. Brenda had been so fortunate to find a clerical job through one of the local job agencies – Swinton Office Services on Station Road.

Albert: Pass me over the teapot, love, and while you're at it another piece of toast.

Brenda: Wait a minute, I just want to have a quick glimpse of the *Journal*.

Albert: You've got all day now, love, to read it… and besides it's only full of photos of weddings, house sales and reports of Swinton Rugby League losing yet again.

Brenda: No, this one is special...because it's got a *Swinton and Pendlebury Journal Centenary Supplement*. Look it's full of local history. Oh, look in here, the first bombing in Swinton was in Wardley in 1940 …and there's an interesting article about Lowry.

Albert: You don't need to tell me about war bombings. Today it's thirty-six years since the start of World War Two. How can any of us forget that?

Brenda sits quietly, skimming over the article about Lowry on page 21, beside a photograph of him taken in 1964, chatting to the mayor of Swinton and Pendlebury, Mrs E Lynch, on a visit to Pendlebury Public Hall.

Brenda: Switch the volume down, love. I want to read this to you.

Albert: I'm enjoying listening to Neil Sedaka, can't it wait until JY has finished?

Brenda: No, otherwise I'll forget when you do the hoovering.

Albert: Alright then, but make it quick, the Carpenters are on next.

Brenda waits and then begins to recite the journal article.

Brenda: Headline: Lowry drew from Acme Mill.

Best known of several artists who have won renown and brought fame to the district is Laurence Stephen Lowry, R.A., who lived on Station Road, Pendlebury before moving to Longdendale in 1948. Whilst his Lancashire industrial scenes have received more publicity, his other paintings of other subjects are equally brilliant. His first local work in his formative period was done around Clifton Junction, and later terraced houses and crofts near Acme Mill, Pendlebury, gave him much inspiration.

Miss Noar: In April 1932 when Lowry had paintings accepted for the Royal Academy, London, another artist from this area, Miss Eva Noar, a native of Swinton also had works on show there ...

Albert: (*interrupts*) very la de dah.

Brenda: Shush, let me finish, I've never heard of this woman before and to think she was a native of Swinton.

The *Journal* stated at that time that 1932 was the 21st year Miss Noar had pictures shown at the Royal Academy, one of her notable commissions being a portrait of the Duchess of Montrose.

Brenda: Ooh, maybe there is something about Miss Noar in the Lancastrian Hall library. Such a lovely building makes you proud to live in Swinton.

Albert: (*smiles*) So can I now go back to listening to Jimmy Young, he's playing the New Seekers.

Brenda: In a mo…the *Journal* article concludes about Lowry, now this I never knew.

Albert: Go on, otherwise I am never going to hear the end of this.

Brenda: Lowry incidentally was made a freeman of Salford in 1965 – an honour overlooked by Swinton and Pendlebury where he has lived so long...

Albert: Typical Salford…and now with this amalgamation of Salford last year, we'll all be the bloody same! Lowry hijacked to Salford and Swinton wiped off the face of the earth.

Brenda: Oh, love, you are being so dramatic, and besides we've got a lovely painting of Lowry, that Patricia gave us for a silver wedding present.

Albert: Yes, and we know what we do with it.

Brenda: Hang it on the lounge wall when we know she is coming to visit.

Albert: I didn't rate Lowry that much, paintings around here in grey, black – with matchstick people. Our lives were not grey and drab, there is beauty in starkness and warmth. Now pass me over that brochure, and I'll be off to Swinton Travel on the Parade to book us a holiday to Torremolinos.

101

Two weeks half board in the sun with pints of Double Diamond on tap.

Brenda: Sounds good to me, this is what retirement is about, enjoying ourselves. Our suitcases are looking a bit rough and scruffy after so many trips to the continent. Let's buy some new luggage from Sinclair-Owen luggage, it is designed and made right here in Swinton – one of Britain's greats in hand luggage. According to the *Journal*.

Albert: OK, but don't go spending all our money at C & A on holiday clothes. You've got a wardrobe full. I blame decimalisation for you spending too much on clobber.

Brenda: I've had enough of reading about Lowry and would much rather have a replica Dali or Picasso from our holidays to Espana, for a few pesetas. Good old General Franco. Spanish paintings are so vibrant and colourful. Who really wants to live in a world of black, white and poverty? Where people worked in mills and factories, down the pit. Glorified and celebrated from a man who once lived in Pendlebury. I wonder, did Lowry ever work in a factory or mill, lose a limb, or clean his front doorstep with a donkey stone? Paintings are an escape – not a reality of the world we knew. Fondness and nostalgia, my arse.

Albert: Watch your language, love. I know what you are like when you've had a couple of glasses of Sangria and cheap Bacardi and Cokes in Spain... and we remember Gaudi's paintings and Franco in the Spanish war. Every painting and artist tells a story...even this one, about Lowry and Miss whoever, in today's *Journal*.

The Visit

Sylvia Edwards

I gaze down from my heavenly place – and smile tenderly. If only he could see me. Sense me. Hear my voice calling out to him. And touch me again. How differently I would return his love and respond to his artistic works. Tears threaten to fall…as raindrops onto the head of my only son: Laurence Stephen Lowry. Oh, how you frustrated me, with your silly, shapeless little figures! I had wanted to see proper human forms: heads, hair, bodies, painted with similarly accurate detail and meaningful expressions…a bit like those the real artistic master, Rembrandt, had produced roughly around three centuries before. Yes, I knew something of art. How my disappointment must have hurt you.

But now…a miracle! Almost unbelievable! Your strange and simple ideas have become renowned works of art. They hang in galleries and people come to view them. Who would have thought it? Oh, Laurence! Laurence! If only I could reach out…and touch you. If only you could sense my pride. I see you now, still sketching those awful places – and the people, with whom you have always seemed obsessed.

And now, I realise, that you, through your unique style of art, have told stories that will stand the test of time. A testament to the lives around which you have always interacted. Salford! What a place: dirty, scruffy, poor. But yet, if you had been born elsewhere, in a posher place, would you have been so inspired?

Can you see me smiling down at you…stretching out my arms towards Earth, about to utter the words I should have uttered many years ago, when you could hear them? *"Well done, my dear son. I am so proud of you."*

Lowry looks up from his sketching of empty houses further down the deserted street. Dilapidated now. A place once so full of vibrant life…now dead. A weird sensation. As if he is

103

being watched. He looks around. No-one. Dusk is falling, as he gathers his pad and pencils. The skin on the back of his neck prickles. He thinks of his mother, Elizabeth. Fancy her having the same name as the Queen – who had wanted to honour him through his art?

Tears threaten. He looks up at the slowly darkening sky. If only his dear mother could see him now – know of his success.

If only…?

Other Publications by SWit'CH

My Life and Other Misadventures   ISBN 978-1-326-60665-7
Alan Rick
A collection of humorous and poignant nostalgic reminiscences covering Alan's early school years in the war to national service in Egypt. Alan looks askance at the society of the day with a wry, knowing, smile.

Switch On, Write On, Read On   ISBN 978-1-326-73048-2
Approx. 200 page the first showcase of the group's creativity. Containing nearly sixty humorous, whimsical, thought-provoking, ironic, and eclectic writing.

A Write Good Read   ISBN 978-0-244-73623-1
Tales from Swinton and Salford; the Wigan train and around the world drawing on the experiences and interests of the group. Modern telecoms and IT feature, so do the Ten Commandments and seven dwarfs. Historical pieces range from the industrial revolution to individual childhood memories.

Peterloo People   ISBN 978-0-244-18472-8
A potpourri of passions gives the reader the chance to walk in those shoes to the peaceful protest, the actions on the day and shameful reaction afterwards. But the focus is not only on the victims; the perspectives of the authorities and militia are treated with sympathy and criticism in due turn – and there's even a wry tale of hope and salvation for a government spy.

A Pain in the Bum   ISBN: 9798590032099
Veronica Scotton
The author's words say it all "I was so very fortunate, not to have to face my cancer alone. Whenever I began to feel overwhelmed, the rock who is my husband was by my side. My children and grandchildren lifted my spirits by being positive about the whole thing and my siblings and friends with their humour, often black humour gave me the best medicine."

Time of the Virus   ISBN 9798541841855
Sylvia Edwards
This book, also supplemented by the authors' poems, short stories and artwork, contains thought-provoking, controversial, views on social inequality, racism, war, religion and politics, encouraging all of us to think hard about what really matters in life.

All Kinds of Everything   ISBN 9798371732019
A collection from the 2023 team of writers. Stories and poetry complemented by members reminiscences. As new members join us, our versatility and variations expand. This collection compares well with the standards established and maintained over the years of the group's successes.

The Taste of Teardrops   ISBN 978-0-244-26569-4
A Novel by Judith Barrie.
A gripping psychological thriller set in a sleepy seaside town. It's 1981 and a young woman settles into her cosy new home believing that she had found peace and tranquillity after a painful marriage break-up. But there are mysteries. Who is the woman upstairs and the irresistibly attractive man who visits her?

Memories Unlocked   ISBN 9798570919617
These childhood reminiscences of localities now gone, holidays, school, nature notes, plane crashes, sex education and walking home after dancing form part of the mischief, mayhem and misadventures of our young lives. Drawn from the experiences of SWit'CH writers in their formative years.

Selected Memories   ISBN 9798598323212
This choice of writers' recollections taken from Memories Unlocked follows on from The Big Switch, which was produced for those with a visual impairment, with a font developed by RNIB. The book is easy to handle. Big letters on low contrast paper make it an easy read and a 'page turner' in the literal sense.

War and Peace in Pludde Bailey   ISBN 979-8391352990
A Novel by Judith Barrie
Pludde Bailey an old fashioned village. There was a public house where men gathered to argue; a corner shop where the women gathered to gossip; a quaint little church up on the hill. Occupied with blackout curtains, rationing and air raid shelters, not one of the inhabitants suspected that they harboured a fledgling killer or that he would kill again nearly twenty years later.

A Lie Never Dies   ISBN: 979-8387509599
A Novel by Sylvia Edwards
1901. This novel charts the dramatic consequences of a lie that drags Kristina through a maze of emotional challenges, changing her life forever. Can she find lasting happiness ina world where she does not belong?

The Big Switch   ISBN : 9798644090433
A collection of short stories in large print format for readers with a visual impairment such as Macular Degeneration or Glaucoma.
'The Big Switch' is a compilation of extracts from some of the group's previously published works. Designed for easy reading.

SPAM   ISBN: 9798879706468
This collection has been collated to showcase the variety and skills of the dynamic writers in and around Swinton, Salford. The sources and prompts for some of the creations are included to demonstrate what stimulates our creativity, whether in-session exercises, 'homeworks' or personal major projects.

Becoming a Reader   ISBN : 9798302216953
Sylvia Edwards
What is reading? Why do we need it? This book explores reading from every perspective;
encouraging all of us - government, teachers, parents, to work together and enable every
child to become an accomplished reader - for life!

How Times Have Changed!   ISBN: 9798877331617
Sylvia Edwards
These memoirs attempt to bridge the post-WW2 world with today's technological version.
Yet, in 2024, as wars still rage, I wonder if humanity is any different than it was - or ever
will be. Against this backdrop, I have told my personal story with honesty and sincerity
and hope that my version of truth reflects what was.

Life Goes On!   ISBN: 9798309412761
Sylvia Edwards
A strange topic to write about you may think. But then is not cancer one of the weirdest
journeys ever undertaken by human beings? Research tells us that one in two are likely
to get some form of cancer in our lifetime. When I first heard this statistic I was aghast -
half of the population! Surely not: that can't be right.
But cancer can have happy endings. Believe it! Beyond the cancer mountain is the
rainbow of hope.

Love, Lies and Loss   ISBN: 9798264870774
Sylvia Edwards
This sequel to A Lie Never Dies follows Kristina into the horrors of the first world war
asshe pursues her quest for happiness. When the past beckons, Kristina needs all her
strength to confront her ghostly memories. Does her new love survive? Can she finally
find herself and the inner peace she craves in the new post-war world?

Printed in Dunstable, United Kingdom

72963458R00067